"I'm not intimidated by your threats."

"David, my business associate, knows all there is to know about client potential...."

"Does he?" Roderick demanded tersely. "Does he also know all there is to know about the woman he wants to marry?" Roderick asked the question fiercely, the burn of his eyes glowing.

"For instance," he said as his fingers swept ruthlessly upward, loosening one hairpin after another until her hair fell in a golden tumble about her shoulders, "does he know you're the most beautiful woman in the world when your hair's down like this? It's like spun gold," he murmured, letting her hair drift sensuously through his hands.

Suddenly Roderick's jaw hardened as he sought the bewildered blue of Fiona's eyes. "Does he ever make love to you like this?"

ELIZABETH GRAHAM
is also the author of these

Harlequin Presents

and these
Harlequin Romances

Many of these books are available at your local bookseller.

For a free catalog listing all titles currently available,
send your name and address to:

HARLEQUIN READER SERVICE
1440 South Priest Drive, Tempe, AZ 85281
Canadian address: Stratford, Ontario N5A 6W2

ELIZABETH GRAHAM

highland gathering

Harlequin Books

TORONTO • NEW YORK • LONDON
AMSTERDAM • PARIS • SYDNEY • HAMBURG
STOCKHOLM • ATHENS • TOKYO • MILAN

Harlequin Presents first edition August 1983
ISBN 0-373-10617-3

Original hardcover edition published in 1983
by Mills & Boon Limited

CHAPTER ONE

'Ask my daughter to come in and see me,' James Mackay instructed his secretary via the intercom, releasing the button without waiting for a reply and swivelling his black leather chair round until he faced the picture windows high above the dark canyons of New York's business district. But it wasn't the shadowy ant-like movements of the traffic thirty floors below that held his attention. His thoughts were more inner-orientated, directed towards the cable lying open on the desk behind him.

'REGRET INFORM YOU THAT YOUR BROTHER FERGUS PASSED AWAY EARLY TODAY PLEASE ADVISE IF ATTENDING FUNERAL FRIDAY NEXT SO ARRANGEMENTS CAN BE MADE MEET YOU IN EDINBURGH. CAIRNS'

Cairns, James mused, the son of the woman Fergus had married after the early death of his first wife. What was the boy's name? Richard ... Robert ... Roderick, that was it. But he wouldn't be a boy now, he'd be a grown man, somewhere in his late twenties, early thirties. He sighed. Was it possible he had never found time to visit his homeland in all those years? He had loved Glenappon, and the castle that had been his home until, the aimless younger son of the Laird, he had shaken the rich soil of Glenappon and Scotland from his serviceable boots and set out to make his fortune in America.

His head turned and he surveyed the evidence of his fruitful quest for fortune. His office was almost an acreage, and it was filled with the best money could buy in paintings, furnishings, plush carpeting. As head of the Mackay hotel chain, these fitted his image. Privately, he still hankered after the scuffed and battered antiques that comprised the furnishing of Glenappon Castle. At today's prices, the armoires and Jacobean chairs, the vast dining table in solid oak and the ancient furnishings of the lofty and draughty main hall would bring a fortune.

A fortune . . . one he didn't need. He had made his money the hard way, though it had been easier to get a foothold then in the post-war boom that swept America. He had started with one run-down hotel in a district that had suddenly become fashionable a year or two after he took it over, and the rest was corporate history. One hotel had led to another, and now he commanded a veritable empire of worldwide hotels known for their appeal to executive tastes. Suites in the Mackay, Florence, boasted prints of that city's most famous art; those at the Mackay, Paris, featured brilliant copies of the French masters; in the United States, each location was authentically represented in the art hanging on its walls. Comfort went hand-in-hand with regional art awareness, and Mackay Hotels had become, over the years, the only place to stay for executives on the go.

So he didn't need the fortune in antiques that Fergus had undoubtedly left him, the sole remaining segment of the Mackays of Glenappon. Fergus had had no children of his own, and James had no sons. There was only. . . .

'I was in a meeting, Dad,' his daughter, Fiona,

said with a tinge of impatience as she walked with her long-limbed suppleness across the vast area of carpet to his desk in front of the windows. 'Carol said you wanted to see me—is it something important? Cal Johnston has to get back to Texas this afternoon, and I was about to question him about the low returns for Dallas in February. I know February isn't the best month anywhere, except in the Caribbean, but——'

'Sit down, Fiona,' James cut into the brittly level voice of his only child. 'I didn't call you in here to talk about business.'

'What?' Fiona stared at him with wide, startled blue eyes, the eyes that so closely resembled his wife's in their crystal Irish depths. Sometimes it pained him to look at his daughter because that eye similarity reminded him of all he had lost when Eleanor died six years before. Nothing else about his daughter served to remind him. Her red-gold hair and stubbornly set chin were all Mackay. Fiona's body was pencil slim, elegant in the well-tailored business suits she favoured, while Eleanor had been small, plump and warm. He worried on occasion that his daughter had sensed his sharp disappointment that she had not been the son he had wanted to follow him in the business, and that she had moulded her personality to conform with what she imagined he would have expected from a son.

'I just got this,' he tossed the cable across the desk, watching the change of her expression from cool detachment to a genuinely warm compassion as he looked up.

'I'm sorry, Dad,' she said softly. 'He was your last link with home, wasn't he?'

'Glenappon is my last link with home,' he

barked in defensive response, then his expression softened when he caught the fleeting look of hurt that was quickly masked on his daughter's face. 'I'm sorry, honey, I can't expect you to understand how I feel about the old place.'

But she did. How could she help knowing when, through the years, his eyes had taken on the desperate longing of the exile, his voice a deeper burr, whenever he told her about his childhood in Scotland? In some ways, Glenappon Castle was as real to her as the Connecticut estate she had grown up on. One day, he had promised her, he would take her to Scotland, to his ancient home. But that day had never come. Somehow there had never been time. She hadn't envisioned their joint trip in such sad circumstances, but. . . .

'Why don't I come along with you?' she suggested with muted pleasure. 'I can clear a couple of weeks from my schedule, and. . . .'

'That's good, honey, because I was going to ask you to go over there and—well, represent this side of the family at the funeral and so on.' Answering his daughter's stunned look, he explained testily, 'You know I can't leave right now with the Florida merger coming to a head. You go ahead and catch the first flight out, and I'll follow you as soon as I can get away.'

Fiona was aghast. All her life she had seen the two of them visiting Scotland together; it had never once occurred to her that she would go alone. 'But—I don't know anybody there,' she protested, 'not even the man whose funeral I'd be attending! Why don't you go and let me negotiate the Florida deal?'

James Mackay's mouth pursed drily. '*You* know you're competent to do that, and *I* know you're competent to do that, but the Mazzini Brothers would never believe in a thousand years that a woman is levelheaded enough to find her way out of the kitchen or—um—the bedroom.' He shrugged. 'It would offend them if I sent you, and I really don't want to do that at this time.'

Railing against the chauvinistic tendencies of the Mazzinis would do nothing to help her, even less her father who, she noticed for the first time, looked more grey and weary than usual. His brother's death must have affected him more than she had imagined it would; he had never spoken of Fergus, his older brother, with warmth or affection. Respect, yes, and a certain amount of awe, but never love ... Fergus was so much older than her father, and the eldest son at that, which meant a lot in the old country.

'Promise you'll come as soon as you can get away?' she accepted the inevitable, rising to stand slim and tall and coolly, despite her colouring, beautiful.

'You can be sure of that.' James rose too and came round the desk to look thoughtfully down at her from his six-feet two inches. 'In fact, I've been wondering if now might not be a good time to let up a little ... maybe a lot. We could bring Glenappon up to date and have most of the comforts we have here, except for theatres and art galleries and things like that, but Edinburgh's only a hundred and ten miles south and it has all the culture you could want. And besides all that,' he enthused, totally disregarding the fact that his daughter, even in Connecticut, had lived an active social life, 'there's miles of heather-covered hills that you can walk all day on and never meet another soul.'

Shock riveted Fiona's eyes on her father's dark brown ones, suddenly lit with an enthusiasm she hadn't seen for a long time ... since her mother had died, in fact. Could he really be considering giving up control of the empire that had been his life's blood for so long? It sounded as if his retirement to Glenappon Castle was something he had long planned ... perhaps he had, just waiting for the demise of his elder brother to put it into operation.

'Dad, don't let's make any hasty decisions,' she said nervously, unable to think at that moment of the meaning such a move would make for her. 'Why don't we wait until we've both been there for a while? Things change over the years, you know, and Glenappon might not be the same to you now as it was when you were a boy. This Cairns man,' she indicated the starkly worded cable, 'could act as manager of the estate for you, and you could visit there as often as you wanted.'

James shook his head emphatically. 'I don't want to be a sometime Laird, I want to live there among my own people and get to know them again. Fergus wasn't the most generous landlord in the world, and I'd like to get to know the people and their needs and do my best to make their lives happier. I have all the money in the world to do just that, and there's really nothing to hold me here ... now.'

His eyes clouded, and Fiona winced. She could make a stab at replacing the son he had never had, but she could never replace the wife he had loved with every fibre of his being.

'All right, Dad,' she agreed quietly, 'I'll go over there and wait for you to come, but,' she paused, 'don't be hurt if I decide not to stay there. My life is here in America; I don't have your memories, all of mine are here.'

James came down from his dream world and gave her an affectionate but shrewd look just before he hugged her. 'Just give it a try, honey, that's all I ask.'

Reaching up, she kissed him on the cheek and turned to leave. 'By the way,' she swivelled back, 'will you let the Cairns man know that I'll be arriving, or should I?'

James frowned dismissingly. 'Oh, Carol will see to it. Just let her know what plane you're catching, and so on.'

Seated comfortably in the first-class section of the transatlantic flight the next morning, Fiona at last had time to relax and mull over her father's decision to become the new Laird of Glenappon. David Warner, his Executive Vice-President of Consumer Relations, had been suitably downcast at the idea of her leaving the United States for an unspecified length of time.

He had even cancelled a promotional meeting with a group of visiting travel agents from around the States in order to drive out to Kennedy airport with her, plying her with reading material as they walked from the lounge to the boarding area. She had felt disorientated somehow, as if she were leaving one life behind and embarking on another, so perhaps her farewell kiss had been warmer than any she had yet bestowed on David. He had been surprised . . . and delighted.

She would probably end up by marrying David, she mused as the plane gathered speed and took off gracefully into the air. He had all the assets a son-in-law of James Mackay required . . . personable, of good family, and almost as enthusiastic as James about the Mackay Hotels chain. Fiona's Scottish canniness had discerned the same ambition in him as she had noted in the many suitors who had ardently sought her since her graduation from the exclusive girls' school in Virginia and on through her university years. They loved her beauty, her cool poise, but even more they had loved the idea of being married to the heiress to the Mackay fortune.

David was different . . . long before he had met her, he had started on a lowly rung of the Mackay empire. If his enthusiasm for the hotel chain had intensified after their first few dates, who could blame him? The prospect of becoming the kingpin one day through his association with the Chairman of the Board's daughter was one no sensible young man would have ignored.

'Would you like a pillow and a blanket?' a passing flight attendant paused to ask, smiling, and Fiona nodded. It would be late evening when she arrived in Edinburgh, and the Cairns man would perhaps want to get back to Glenappon that same night.

As she settled back into her seat under the blanket, her thoughts veered from David to the man who would be awaiting her arrival. Roderick Cairns.

What would he be like? Would he resent her, the daughter of a younger son who was, nevertheless, heir to Glenappon Castle and all it entailed? Falling into a restless sleep, she wondered just how resentful the son of her uncle's second wife might be of a usurping American and his family. An American who had, moreover, not set foot in his native land since his departure from it thirty-odd years before.

She surprised herself, sleeping through the meal service and awaking only when the attendant touched her shoulder and informed her that they would be landing at Edinburgh in twenty minutes. Fiona sat up and relinquished the blanket and pillow, staggering along to the small toilet compartment and staring at her unfamiliarly unkempt appearance in the small mirror above an even smaller sink.

Swiftly she rinsed her face and applied new make-up, then smoothed the bright red-gold strands of her hair back into the chignon she had worn for the past four years. It was an easy style to care for, and one that inspired confidence in business associates.

After New York's June heat, the air struck cool when she stepped from the plane, and she was glad of the camel cape-style coat clinging heavily round her shoulders. Immigration and Customs procedures were no more boring than they ever were when she travelled, but this time she was irritably tired, despite her catnap on board.

'You're here for a visit, Miss Mackay?' the immigration officer asked in a soft Scottish sing-song accent that somehow made her feel unbearably alien.

'Yes, I am.'

'And how long would you be intending to stay?'

'I really have no idea,' she snapped, then elaborated more amenably, 'I'm here to attend the funeral of my uncle—Fergus Mackay of Glenappon?' she told him with the surety that in such a small country everyone would know everyone else.

'I see,' he said in an impersonal tone that told her he had never heard of Glenappon or the demise of its master. 'Well, if you'll just step over there, Miss Mackay,' he indicated a further row of Dickensian type desks, 'you'll talk to the Customs people and then you'll be free to go. Are you being met?'

'Yes, I am. Thank you.'

Fiona dragged her luggage before the impersonal eyes of the Customs inspector and reiterated her statements to the tired and obviously bored official there. Then at last she was free, and she emerged into the arrival hall, her eyes searching futilely for the Cairns man. She had no idea what he looked like; short, tall, dark, fair. Wearily, she wished that Carol, her father's secretary, had arranged for him to be wearing a sign, as so many chauffeurs seemed to, declaring 'FORSDYKE', 'HARRISON', 'MAKINTOSH'. Patience ebbed when all these were claimed, and she scanned again the thinning crowd of welcomers. Time after time, expectant looks were transformed into smiles of welcome, yet no one came forward to claim her as a longed-for visitor.

Finally, only an austere-looking man, dressed incredibly in a kilt, was left in the reception area. Tall, dark, austere in tweed jacket above the muted colours of his kilt, which left a brawny expanse of knee exposed until tartan socks discreetly covered swelling calves and thin-boned ankles, he was the personification of all she had dreamed of in Scottish men. He was so true to life that she felt faint as he walked impatiently towards her, his dark eyes flashing awareness, then his steps carried on past her to the official she had last seen.

He talked briefly with the official, then turned to look at her as the man pointed in her direction.

Lethargy fled from her when their eyes met, his a stormily remote brown, hers a fascinated blue. Her senses seemed to prickle into deeper awareness when he strode towards her.

'I was expecting to meet Mr James Mackay,' he said in a hard accent that nonetheless betrayed his highland origin.

'That—that's my father,' she stammered as gauchely as she had at the age of fourteen. 'He's—coming later. I'm Fiona Mackay.' She put out an automatic hand, and he looked at it for several seconds before engulfing it with his own long, fine-boned fingers.

'The telegram said that James Mackay would be arriving by this flight,' he said accusingly as he dropped her hand and stared at her intently.

'There must have been some mistake,' she floundered, desperately summoning up her normal coolness. 'His secretary——'

'Am I to understand that James Mackay will be arriving by a later flight?'

Fiona looked up into the eyes that were two or three inches above her father's, and felt a return of her normal calm when she said, 'My father will be coming as soon as he concludes some very important business. I'm standing in for him, and——' she flicked the dark brown eyes with her own, 'I'll come back to pick him up myself, so you don't have to worry about making a second journey.'

'That wasn't my worry,' he retorted coolly, bending to pick up the largest of her suitcases in one hand and lifting the other as if it weighed nothing at all. 'I had arranged a double room in Edinburgh before setting out for Glenappon, but of course that is now out of the question.' He walked ahead, as if the heavy suitcases were feather-light bundles of hay . . . or heather.

Fiona drew to an abrupt halt and twisted her head to look up at his forbidding expression. 'You mean you've already booked accommodation in Edinburgh?'

'Of course. But it's not suitable accommodation for two people of the—er—opposite sex travelling together.'

He sounded so like her father that Fiona almost laughed. Roderick Cairns wasn't the man she would have chosen to spend an illicit night in a hotel with, but the prospect of setting out on a journey over second-grade roads wasn't one she relished in her overtired state. So what if they had to share a communal living room, even a bathroom, in the hotel he had booked? She was bone-weary, tired to the point of exhaustion after letting up on the tension that normally kept her going.

'Just lead me to it,' she said wearily, following him as he passed through the outer doors to the kerbside, where a battered jeep-type vehicle reposed in solitary splendour.

'I think your father would not like the thought that you will be spending the night in my company,' her stalwart escort intoned as he competently set the vehicle in motion and rocketed away from the airport confines.

'My father only cares about my wellbeing,' she retorted wryly as he turned left on to the highway, 'and at this moment, my wellbeing consist of a good night's sleep before—look out!' she screeched before remembering that traffic drove on the left here as in England. The truck she had thought was bearing down on them passed innocuously to their right and thundered down into the night. 'I'm sorry,' she addressed the forbidding profile, 'I haven't found my road-feet yet.'

Her answer was a taciturn grunt, and no more words were exchanged between them until the vehicle pulled up to the side of a hotel looking out on a tranquil square in Edinburgh itself.

'I'll go in and see that the booking is all right,' Roderick Cairns said in a strained voice as he got out and looked up at the sand rock building before them. 'You stay here until I come back.'

Leaving her no other option, he strode majestically off in the direction of the pillared entrance. Leaning back against the worn leather of the less-than-comfortable passenger seat, Fiona watched him go, his kilt swinging under rigidly flat hips. Did he really believe that a hotel in this modern twentieth century would object if two unmarried people shared a suite?

Evidently he did think so, for even after checking in at the desk he came back to usher her hurriedly and secretively into an ancient elevator that bore them gruntingly up to the fourth floor. It would be amusing, she thought, if she wasn't so darned tired. Jet lag wasn't a figment of the psychologists' imaginations. She felt drained of energy and power when her escort led her into a room cosily furnished with chintzy curtains and twin beds delicately turned back to invite deep, dreamless sleep.

'This is fine,' Fiona said approvingly after surveying the room. 'Where are you going to be?'

Their eyes locked for a moment, then, sensing his embarrassment, she moved further into the room and threw her briefcase and bag on to the nearest bed.

'I'm going to be here, with you,' he said stiffly, still standing by the outer door. 'I thought you understood that this room had been booked for—your father and myself.'

Curse Carol! How could she have made a mistake like this? A suite with two bedrooms and a communal living room was one thing—this unexpected intimacy was another. One of the beds stared accusingly back at her as her eyes flicked over it. It, like the stalwart Scot holding up the far wall, probably expected an American morals-be-damned orgy on its chaste floral spread.

'Look, Mr—er—Cairns?' she began 'whatever you may believe about swinging America, I'm not part of it. Why don't you find yourself another room?'

The dark eyes glinted frostily. 'There's none available, I've already made enquiries.' As if reading her transparent thought, he added drily, 'Spending the night on a sofa in the hotel lounge would be the gallant thing to do, but it's more important that I get a good night's rest before driving back to Glenappon in the morning. I can assure you that you will not be—troubled.' His mouth closed tightly over the last words, and Fiona stifled a giggle born of hysteric tiredness.

'All right,' she capitulated with weary lack of interest, turning to unzip her travel bag, 'do I use the bathroom first or do you?'

He was silent for so long that she swung back to stare at him curiously and surprised a dark flush on the lean weathered cheeks. 'I'll go down and get my things from the car while you use it,' he said starkly, and Fiona found herself staring at the door instead as he made a hasty retreat.

Was he really, at his age and with his apparent

confidence otherwise, inexperienced and shy with women? No, he couldn't be, she decided ... not with those dark attractive looks and that air of aloof brooding that always attracted women in droves. Even the proud hook of his nose under the thick brows and deep-set dark eyes added to rather than detracted from his appearance. Shrugging, she pulled out the nightdress and toiletries she always carried in the travel bag on the plane with her, and made her way into the small bathroom.

Although she was too weary to rush, she was already safely under the covers of the bed closest to the windows when he came back. Despite the lamp between the beds shining directly into her eyes, she was almost asleep and it was too much trouble to force her eyes open or speak. She heard a soft rustle of movement, then the light snapped off.

Tired as she was, she dreamed in jumbled snatches. All she could remember when she woke was that there had been dark buildings and a dark man on horseback who snatched her up and galloped off with her along cobbled city streets.

A weak sun struggled against the net curtains at the unfamiliar windows and she glanced at her watch, which was still on her wrist. It read two-thirty ... heavens, had she slept right through till afternoon? Remembering her unlikely companion of the night, she jerked her head in the direction of the neighbouring bed and saw with mingled feelings that it was empty, though it had been slept in.

Had Cairns grown disgusted with her lateness and left her to find her own way back to Glenappon? It seemed like something the taciturn Scot would do, she judged sourly, throwing back the covers. She had obviously been right about his resenting the American Mackays taking over Glenappon, but he'd find out he couldn't get rid of them that easily! She would rent a car and drive up there herself . . . a knock sounded at the door and she leapt back under the covers, her face already composed into cold disdain for the man who hadn't, after all, abandoned her.

The look was lost on the cheerful, round and healthy red face of the black-clad maid who entered bearing a tray loaded with silverware pots and jugs and plate covers.

'Good morning, ma'am.' She settled the tray over the startled Fiona's knees and smiled shyly as her eyes went over the long stream of red-gold hair tumbling over Fiona's pale-skinned shoulders, bare apart from the shoestring straps of her filmy pale blue nightdress. 'It's a beautiful day, nice and sunny and warm.' Her accent was thick, but more level than the Immigration man's of the evening before.

'I'd no idea I'd slept so long!' Fiona exclaimed, glancing again at her watch, then remembering that the maid had greeted her with a 'Good morning'. Of course! Her watch was still set on New York time, so it was two-thirty in the morning there, a reasonable seven-thirty a.m. here.

'Och, it's early yet,' the maid dismissed, 'though the gentleman does seem to be in a hurry to get away. He was down asking for his breakfast just after six.'

Man of action! Fiona lifted the cover from the largest plate and gasped. 'I can't eat all this at this time of the day!' In addition to thick-sliced ham and fried eggs, grilled tomato halves decorated the plate and alternating slices of black and white pâté-like circles loaded the plate to overflowing. 'What's that?'

'Black pudding, and the other is white pudding,' the maid explained, obviously amused at Fiona's ignorance. 'The black pudding is made of blood and——'

'Don't tell me any more!' Fiona shuddered, replacing the lid on the congealing breakfast. 'I'll just have the toast and coffee.'

'The gentleman thought you would prefer tea,' the maid said in a less friendly tone, 'but I can bring you coffee if you want it.'

Fiona hastily picked up the teapot and began to pour the almost black liquid into the capacious cup. 'No, don't bother, tea will be fine. Thanks.'

She didn't linger over breakfast. The toast, in a slotted holder, was cold and tough and the tea lukewarm and bitter. Besides, she reminded herself, disgruntled, 'the gentleman' was anxious to get away.

Roderick Cairns was waiting impatiently in the lobby when she went down thirty minutes later. He was dressed in the same as the night before; the only difference was that his broad-set chin was slightly less dark, his black hair brushed more neatly. How could she not have heard the sounds of his shaving through the thin wall separating bed and bathroom? The reality of having shared her bedroom with this formidable stranger suddenly hit her, and warm colour surged under her cheeks as he strode towards her, kilt swinging.

'Good morning.'

For a moment Fiona thought he was about to shake hands formally, which would have looked ridiculous to the curious clerk eyeing them from behind the scarred reception desk, so she slid her right hand down over the strap of her travel bag and closed it over the zipper area. There was more tart irony in her voice than she had intended when she said, 'I'm sorry if I've kept you waiting, I don't usually sleep so late.'

'That's all right. It's understandable you'd be tired after such a long journey.'

Fiona sensed that something in his attitude had changed overnight, but she couldn't put her finger on where the change lay. Maybe it was just that she was seeing things clearer after the night's rest.

'I'll arrange for your luggage to be brought down,' he said with more warmth than he had shown so far, and Fiona cursed her own competence when she called him back in the middle of a forceful stride towards the desk.

'I—already did that.'

He frowned. 'Oh? Well then, we'll get right off as soon as it gets here.'

'Does it take so long to travel a hundred and ten miles in Scotland?' she asked, irritated at having been put on the defensive.

'No. It's just that I have an appointment that I can't miss this afternoon.'

He sighted her suitcase then, and moments later they were descending the hotel steps to the waiting vehicle at the kerb. He was polite as he opened the passenger door for her, but untalkative when they left the quiet square and drove several blocks before coming to a main thoroughfare, where they were halted by red traffic lights.

'This is Princes Street,' he explained in a neutral voice. 'I thought you'd like to take a drive along it before we leave Edinburgh.'

'Thanks, I would.' Surprised by his thought-fulness, Fiona sat back and let her entranced eyes take in the broad street lined with what seemed quality stores on one side, parks and gardens on the other. Dominating it all was the stark-faced Castle perched high up on craggy rocks, and Fiona drew in her breath in sharp awareness. Her father had filled her with romantic tales of Edinburgh Castle's history and she had always felt she would be no stranger to it when finally she saw it, but nothing compared to this gasping awe that filled her throat. It was remote, majestic, broodingly protective and totally magnificent.

They were on their way out of the city when she found her voice again. 'I always imagined Glenappon Castle would be just like the pictures I saw of Edinburgh Castle, but it's not—is it?'

He astounded her by throwing his head back and laughing aloud. Glancing at him, she saw a totally different man. Gone was the heavy seriousness, and he looked years younger as his eyes sparkled with warmth, creasing easily into the laughter lines surrounding them which she hadn't noticed before. The firm set of his mouth relaxed and revealed regular, very white teeth. He should laugh more often, she thought, her own mouth curving infectiously. Dourly good looking in his normal state, now he was positively devastating.

'Have you never seen photographs of Glenappon?' he asked, brows lifted over still-smiling eyes.

'No, Dad didn't have any. He wrote Uncle Fergus and asked for some once years ago, but——'

'Well, I can assure you it's nothing like Edinburgh,' he broke in as if uninterested in hearing about Fergus's unbrotherly coolness. 'For one thing, Glenappon is much later than

Edinburgh Castle, only about three hundred years old, and it hasn't always been occupied by Mackays. In fact, they've only been there for a hundred and fifty or so years. The original Alistair Mackay of Glenappon came by it in an odd way. He——'

'Yes, I know,' she interrupted, irritated by his assumption that she needed a stranger to tell her about her ancestry, 'he won it and the owner's daughter in a gambling game. It's the castle itself I'm vague about.'

Sober again, he glanced at her thoughtfully then bent his eyes on the road once more. 'It's more of a country house than a castle,' he explained levelly, 'though it has a tower that gives a view of the whole surrounding country, so that there could never be an unexpected attack. The walls are thick and made of local stone, as are the floors on the ground level. There are thirty bedrooms arranged in two wings, and there's been little modernisation there apart from wood flooring and two or three additional bathrooms. Your uncle wasn't one for entertaining on a large scale,' he ended on a dry note which implied that Fergus Mackay hadn't entertained on any scale at all.

'What was he like, my uncle?' Fiona asked impulsively. If anyone knew him, this man did. He had lived with her uncle at Glenappon from the time he was a boy. Somehow no clear picture of Fergus had come through from her father's brief descriptions of him.

'Fergus?' His eyes narrowed thoughtfully. 'Like most of us, he was a mixture. He could be kind and considerate; he could also be cold and unapproachable.'

'Which was he to you?'

He was silent for a moment or two, negotiating a bend on the narrow road they had turned off on before replying. Then his answer was brief, laconic. 'Sometimes one, sometimes the other. Mostly he was good to me, saw that I had the best education to fit me for my chosen profession.'

Fiona stared at him in surprise. Why had she imagined that he had simply loafed around the castle living high off her uncle's hog?

'Profession?'

He glanced at her again. 'You sound surprised. I'm a structural engineer. I'd just completed a contract in Saudi Arabia when Fergus became ill. My mother asked me to stay until—it was over, and I did.'

Another shockwave hit Fiona. She hadn't given one thought to the woman who had been Fergus's second wife. Yet within a matter of hours she would be meeting the mother of this inexplicable man.

'I guess,' she ventured tentatively, 'your mother is pretty much in shock right now.'

His sparsely fleshed hands seemed to tighten on the wheel. 'She expected it,' he said abruptly. 'Fergus had been ailing off and on for a long time.'

'Oh.'

Was she as soberly unemotional as her son? What was her name? Fiona racked her brains for the next few miles, only partially aware of the small, secretive-looking villages they passed through, the change from rolling foothills to fir-clad slopes and stark rocky peaks. Had she ever known the name of her uncle's second wife?

The silence that fell between them seemed a natural thing, and Fiona half-dozed as they traversed the sparsely travelled road winding through the hills. Sheep cropped intently at the lower slopes where, she suspected, heather would cover the hills with a reddish-purple haze later in the season. The mystery was that anything flourished at all on those stark mountainsides after such intense grazing, but she knew from her father that they would indeed blaze with colour in August and September.

Where would she be by then? Back in New York holding the reins for her father who had decided to become a Laird in his late middle age? Planning her marriage to David, looking for a suitable apartment not too far from the Mackay Hotels building? The fumes and noise of New York's traffic obtruded noxiously on the silent splendour surrounding her, and she blocked it from her mind. Her eyes fixed on the bony knuckled hands of the man beside her as they grasped the wheel were the last things she saw as she nodded frankly to sleep.

CHAPTER TWO

THE drawing of the car to one side and the sudden quiet as the engine was cut off brought Fiona back to dazed reality. Blinking, she sat up from her slumped position, thankful that she hadn't succumbed in sleep to that broad, inviting shoulder so close to her own. She could see that there was still only wild country surrounding them, not the castle she had expected.

'What's wrong?' she asked, blinking sleep from

her eyes as she looked into the unfathomable depths of Roderick Cairns's.

'Nothing,' he said with a husky intensity she missed for the moment. 'I just thought you would like to be awake when we come into Glenappon.'

'Oh.' Again he had proved unusually thoughtful. 'Thank you, it does mean a lot to me.'

'I guessed that.' He paused. 'I also wanted to ask you not to tell my mother that we shared a hotel room last night. She might not understand.'

His mother might not understand?—or the woman he had an appointment with that afternoon? She had already decided that only a woman would dredge that much punctiliousness from a man like Roderick Cairns.

'I won't breathe a word,' she promised lightly, her hands busily smoothing the red-gold strands of her hair back into the chignon. 'How do I look? Fit for a triumphal homecoming?' His long silence made her want to snatch the words back. In the circumstances, they had been distasteful in the extreme.

'You look beautiful enough for anything,' he said slowly, astonishingly. Her arms still raised to her head, Fiona swivelled round to look at him. 'But you're a lot more beautiful with your hair down as it was last night in bed.'

Still grappling with the notion that he had watched her while she slept, Fiona was unprepared for the reach of his fingers for the pins confining her hair, the almost sensual pleasure he took in running his fingers through it when it tumbled round her shoulders. What stunned her most of all, however, was when his palms cupped her cheeks and drew her head the short distance to where his mouth waited to commandeer hers in a kiss that shook her in its unexpectedness. There was nothing especially passionate about it, just a confident assertion of—possession?

'What did you do that for?' She struggled easily away from him, her eyes sparking blue fire as they met the good-humoured brown of his. 'I told you I'm not one of the swinging generation!'

'I didn't hear too much about any generation, swinging or otherwise, in Saudi Arabia,' he retorted drily, but smiling almost against his will. Softly, he added, 'I just wanted to kiss you, is that so bad?'

'It is when we'd never laid eyes on each other until last night,' she snapped, straightening with a jerk and tossing her bright mane of hair back over her shoulders. 'I think you'd better drive on,' she said frigidly.

He spent another few moments staring at her, then she felt rather than saw him shrug, and the engine hummed to life once more. She was so incensed that the huddle of grey rock cottages that comprised the village of Glenappon slid past without her noticing them. Who did he think he was, to force his unwanted kisses on her? Primed by all the men who had preceded him, she didn't have to look too far. He wanted Glenappon, and the only way he would get it was through the daughter of the new Laird. How sick she was of men who used every power in the sexual handbook to gain their own ends! Well, he would find that she wasn't so easily won over with a kiss or a hug. She was in the driver's seat; she didn't need him or any other man to pursue her life of independence. Except perhaps for—

She leaned forward in her seat and forgot everything else when the vehicle rose from the huddled cottages below along a winding upward road and revealed tempting glimpses through the towering firs of weathered stone thrusting up towards a pale blue sky. Round a bend in the gravelled drive, the whole building burst into view and left her breathless. Was it possible that she was here at last at Glenappon, reality far superseding the hazy conception she had nurtured from childhood?

It seemed immense as the vehicle's wheels crunched on the gravelled forecourt and drew up at the central iron-studded door above a broad sweep of shallow stone steps. Reality was so much more overwhelming than her hazy conception of her father's birthplace that she sat and stared openmouthed until her companion of hours came and opened her door, touching her arm with his fingertips to remind her that she should make that one last journey into the home of her fathers.

The heavy door swung open when she had barely made her faltering way up the steps, and a small plump woman dressed simply in heather-toned skirt and lilac blouse, came to stand on the paved terrace outside the entrance. Fiona had a fleeting impression of greying brown hair, bright warm dark eyes, a softly welcoming body as she was enfolded to the woman in an intimate embrace.

'Oh, my dear,' she said warmly, standing back with her hands still on Fiona's arms, 'I'm so happy to welcome you to Glenappon!'

Not sure whether she rightfully should, Fiona forced a smile and thanked her. She had, after all, more right to be here than Roderick Cairns or his mother.

'Come away in,' the homely woman pressed

excitedly, pulling Fiona over the threshold into an enclosed stone-flagged porch that opened out further on to an immense hall lit by dusty beams of sunlight from narrow windows set high up in the bare rock walls. If she disapproved of Fiona's well-cut pants suit in soft blue polyester, she gave no sign of it. She left Fiona momentarily to greet her son with a fond peck on his cheek.

'How did you know that it's James's daughter and not himself who was arriving from America?' he echoed Fiona's inner question.

'Och, I had a telephone call from James himself,' she divulged dismissingly. 'He wanted to make sure you'd be welcomed fittingly, my dear,' she addressed Fiona brightly, 'as if we wouldn't have anyway.' Her animated face darkened momentarily. 'How Fergus would have loved to see his only niece! And you so bonny, too.'

'Mother, I think Fiona would like to see her room now,' her son reminded her tactfully, and Fiona felt a tug of pleasurable surprise at the way he said her name.

'Yes, of course. This way, my dear.' The older woman stepped briskly into the main hall and approached a stone staircase situated halfway along it and clothed in worn blue carpeting. 'Fergus was always talking about buying new carpet for the stair,' she divulged, 'but somehow it never seemed to come to pass.'

'It never came to pass, Mother,' her son reminded her drily from below, 'because it needed more money than the estate could supply!'

'Now, Roderick, don't be bothering the girl with things she knows nothing about,' his mother retorted sharply, panting slightly as they neared the upper gallery which overlooked the hall below. 'Your room is this way, my dear.'

Fiona, disorientated in time and space, automatically followed the matronly figure along the corridor that branched right from the upper hallway. Her mind was more totally occupied with the fact that even his mother addressed him by his full name—not Roddy, or even Rod, but Roderick.

The room she was shown into had all the charm and character Americans sought after but seldom attained. An ancient four-poster bed dominated the room, its rich blue and gold embroidered coverlet conjuring up royal days long past. Broad window seats, padded and covered with the same blue and gold-thread that adorned the bed's coverlet, displayed through leaded glass triangular panes the misty outline of lawns and rosebeds, shrubbery and small trees in varied shades of green.

'It's beautiful!' Fiona breathed, sinking down on one of the window seats to stare out at the view. 'I feel as if I belong here.'

'Well now, that's not surprising,' the older woman observed brightly as she came to stand beside Fiona. 'Your father was brought up here, and I don't doubt told you a lot about it.'

'Yes, he did,' Fiona confirmed softly. 'But I'd no idea I would really find it as beautiful as he said it was.'

'Things seldom are,' the older woman agreed sagely, then seemed to draw herself up. 'Well now, my dear, you'll want to get ready for lunch. It will be served in thirty minutes—will that be enough time for you to get settled in?'

'I'm sure it will. Thank you, Mrs——' She

paused. 'Mrs Mackay' was too formal, and it reminded her of her mother.

'Oh, just call me Isabel,' the other woman said airily as she turned away. 'Everybody calls me that except Roderick. I wouldn't mind the more modern way, but he's just a bit old-fashioned, so he sticks to "Mother". I'll see you soon, then.'

Old-fashioned! Fiona smiled as she watched Isobel Cairns go to the door. She'd noticed how old-fashioned her son was! He was obviously the light in his mother's eye—did the older woman resent the alien American, James Mackay, becoming the new Laird of Glenappon? She had to . . . if not for her own sake, then for her son's.

Sighing, Fiona rose from the window seat and investigated her room. Heavy antique furniture comprised the necessary chests of drawers, massive wardrobes, dressing table, stools. There was even an overstuffed seating arrangement of small sofa and two armchairs round a corner fireplace—but no adjoining bathroom. Investigating the wide corridor, carpeted in faded paisley, the third door she opened revealed a massive scrolled-feet tub, single pedestal sink, a white-painted dressing table with mirror fastened separately to the wall above, an abundance of towel rails and one complete wall of white painted floor-to-ceiling cupboards. Everything needed to complete her toilette was neatly placed in appropriate spots. Like the bedroom, it had an air of quiet waiting as if the present occupant was transiently unimportant in the long scheme of things.

Walking along the corridor towards the stair twenty minutes later, glancing at the occasional suits of armour and the more regularly appearing portraits of past Mackays, she reflected idly that the castle would make a fantastic hotel. Not for the usual executive types the chain normally catered to, but for all those Americans who had roots here in Scotland, who would like nothing better than to spend a week or two in such authentic surroundings. Not quite as authentic as they were at the moment, she corrected herself mentally, avoiding a treacherous threadbare patch of carpet on the broad sweep of stairs. It would need a lot of money to bring it up to scratch, but her father didn't have to worry about that. . . .

Her father! Hotel man though he was, he would never consider turning his family heritage into a tourist resort. This was the one place in the whole world where he could be himself, know who he was.

The vast hall was empty of people, though she heard faint sounds as from a kitchen towards the rear. Curious, she crossed the stone flags to one of the heavy black doors positioned to one side of a massive fireplace made of rock. The door swung open with surprising ease when she touched the handle and she peered round it, her eyes widening at the room's size and ornately heavy grandeur. Another rock fireplace dominated the far wall with chintz-covered furniture surrounding it, glass-fronted cabinets scattered here and there displaying she knew not what. There would be time later to investigate more thoroughly, and she closed the door, deciding to find the dining room.

At the other end of the hall another door attracted her and she walked more boldly into this room, halting when she saw that it was mainly in darkness. Was this one of the many rooms that must have been closed off as entailing too much upkeep, as many of the castle rooms must be? But no ... she could see from the sunlight struggling through the ill-fitting blinds that the furniture was unshrouded, and sensed that it was a room well used normally. Its dim outlines told her that it was a smaller room than the one she had just come from, though that impression was probably emphasized by the dimly solid mass at its centre. Reinforcing her surmise was the strong scent of flowers in the room. . . .

'Is somebody in here?'

Fiona blinked as overhead lights flashed on, her eyes having become accustomed to the pall-like gloom of the room. 'It's only me——' She started to swing round, then stood transfixed with widening eyes on the central arrangement of furniture. Low tables supported a brass-embellished black coffin, the flowers she had smelled arranged fulsomely in vases at either end. Inside the open coffin she glimpsed the stark outlines of an aged face, and for the first time in her life she screamed in terror, her knees buckling under her.

'It's all right, it's all right!' Strong arms were holding her, and her face was pressed to the harsh tweed of Roderick Cairns's jacket.

'Oh no,' she moaned, shuddering. 'I didn't know he would be—here!'

'It's customary.' Fingers she would remember later as being incredibly gentle pressed under her chin until her horror-filled eyes lifted to his. 'I didn't know that you would come wandering in here on your own, but now that you are here, perhaps you should say hail and farewell to your uncle.'

Fiona's lids closed. 'That's barbaric,' she whispered. 'I—I couldn't!'

'We're known as a barbaric people. We're also

known,' he added softly, 'as fiercely loyal to kin and country. Fergus Mackay is your kin in death as he was in life, and I think you may have regrets later if you shirk from this now. Look at him, Fiona,' he turned her in his arms and held on to her, ignoring her tightly closed eyes as he went on, 'he's no better and no worse than he was in life. All you will see is a man who lived long and well, a man now at peace with his Maker.'

Knowing she would have fallen had it not been for the warm security of his arms around her, his body behind her, Fiona blinked her lids open. Her eyes focused reluctantly on the proud, craggy profile with its wax-like skin stretched over high-bridged nose and prominently marked cheeks. A sandy-grey, clipped moustache matched the thinning hair on his head and gave him a human touch so real that she could almost imagine his drily humorous expression in life. There was nothing ... absolutely nothing ... fearsome about her deceased uncle. He looked supremely at peace, as Roderick had said.

Turning in his arms without loosening them, she looked up into his eyes and said simply, 'Thank you.' He seemed about to say something in reply when his mother's voice sounded from the open doorway.

'Oh, you're in here! Roderick, you might have waited until after lunch, the poor girl must be starved. Come away now, or Maggie will be throwing pots around all afternoon!'

Isabel Cairns seemed not to notice the intimate clasp of her son's arms round the slender waist of her late husband's niece. Nor did she seem unduly distraught by the so recent demise of that husband. Maybe Scottish women were more practical than their American counterparts, and didn't waste time in futile regrets when life was still there for them to live.

The dining room was at the opposite end of the large entrance hall, a sombre place oppressively furnished with dark mahogany sideboards and a table laid for three which would have seated forty without crowding. Thin Gothic style windows provided a distorted view of a rose garden through their leaded panes, and again there was a trunk-sized fireplace strategically placed to warm diners at the centre of the long, rectangular table. A plump girl dressed in dark blue with white half-apron served what would have been the evening meal in America. Roast beef, which Roderick at the head of the table carved into thick slices, accompanied by individual puddings and a nondescript leafy green vegetable. Dessert was a pink-coloured custard that tasted synthetic.

Conversation was minimal during the meal, and Fiona was glad of that. She was still shaking inside from that shockingly sudden view of her uncle's body. If it hadn't been for Roderick Cairns . . . she glanced at the profile to her right, finding it intent on swallowing the meal as quickly as was polite. The woman he had the appointment with must be somebody special, she thought with an odd pang. However, Isabel's next words proved how wrong her emotional judgment had been.

'I'm sure Craig won't bother if you're a few minutes late in seeing him,' she observed with a frown to her uncommunicative son. To Fiona she explained, 'Craig Jameson is the factor for the estate, and Roderick promised to go and look at some trees that are ailing over at—well, at the other side of Glenappon Loch.' She looked again at her son. 'I would have thought that a few doubtful trees could have waited until after ... after.'

He gave her a dry smile. 'The pine fly bothering the trees unfortunately takes no account of the affairs of men. Fergus's death won't make one bit of difference to their destructive tendencies.' Seeming to recall Fiona's naïveté on estate matters, he turned to her and explained, 'Most of Glenappon's prosperity lies in the pine forests, so it's a matter of grave concern that the trees are in danger of being destroyed. Craig Jameson needs my opinion as to whether widespread spraying is required.'

His opinion! He sounded as if he were the master of all he surveyed, and Fiona resented that on her father's behalf. She had no time to verbalise her thoughts, however, for he wiped his mouth hastily with his white linen napkin and pushed his chair back.

'I shouldn't be too long,' he addressed his mother, 'but have your tea if I'm not back by four.' Nodding to Fiona, he strode out of the room—this time, she noticed belatedly, wearing thick tweed trousers in place of the kilt. It made no appreciable difference to the taut confidence of his hips.

'Your son certainly seems to be knowledgeable in more than one area,' Fiona remarked probingly into the small silence that followed his departure, and Isabel smiled with motherly pride.

'He is that. Roderick is very much in demand as an engineer, you know, in many parts of the world, but his real love is Glenappon. Fergus relied on him so much, and he was sorely grieved when Roderick accepted the job in Saudi Arabia.

In some ways, of recent years, he was regarded more as the Laird than Fergus himself.'

'Really?' Fiona asked in a cool voice that Isabel missed. 'So why did he go to Saudi Arabia?'

'Oh,' the older woman shrugged, pouring tea from the large pot the girl had brought, 'Fergus didn't agree with some of Roderick's plans for Glenappon, they quarrelled and Roderick went off for three years. Do you take milk and sugar in your tea, Fiona?'

Fiona didn't normally take tea. But coffee was obviously a rare drink in this country, so she supposed she'd better get used to the thick black brew. 'Both, please.' Her brain was busy registering what Isabel had told her when the door burst open and a whirling burst of energy catapulted into the room in the shape of a small-statured dark girl with healthily flushed cheeks and inquisitive brown eyes. She seemed disappointed to find only the two women finishing lunch.

'Oh.' Her eyes flicked from her encompassing look at Fiona to settle on the older woman. 'I thought Roderick would be here. He promised to take me to see old Mrs Anderson when he went.' Her voice was high-pitched, but it had an attractive accent. She was dressed in clothes that became her sturdy figure ... beige-coloured loosely fitting twill slacks and yellow blouse topped by a thick-knit sweater.

Isabel regarded the disappointed girl, who was a few years younger than Fiona, with a tolerant smile. 'Roderick has found more urgent calls on his time than visiting Mrs Anderson. Let me introduce you to our guest, Miss Fiona Mackay.' To Fiona she said, 'This is Catriona Baird, her father manages one of the Glenappon farms.'

Fiona sensed an emotional wall between herself and the other girl as she nodded to her, and wondered, amused, if she imagined Fiona as a rival for the affections of the dour Roderick Cairns.

'You live in a very beautiful part of the world,' she said genially, and saw the younger girl frown uncertainly.

'You sound like an American,' she blurted in a puzzled tone.

'That's not surprising ... I am American, though Fergus Mackay was my father's brother. This is my first visit to Scotland.'

'So you're not ...' Catriona left the sentence unfinished, but her eyes sought confirmation from Isabel.

'Fiona is part of the family,' the older woman said evenly, rising and picking up her untouched cup of tea, smiling slightly in Fiona's direction as she added, 'Will you excuse me if I leave you now? I always have a rest after lunch.'

'Surely,' Fiona hastened to assure her, though she wasn't too sure about being left in the company of a girl who kept sliding curiously speculative looks at her.

'Oh, don't worry, Mrs Mackay, I'll stay with her till Roderick comes back.'

'Yes ... well, I'll be down in good time for tea.'

The younger girl looked like an animal stalking its prey as Isabel went from the room, and she walked on booted feet round the table to take the place of the older woman with a confidence Fiona found objectionable.

'Why did you come here?' Catriona asked insolently, emphasising her familiarity with the house by reaching for the pot and pouring tea into the cup that would have been Roderick's had he stayed.

'I would have thought that was obvious,' Fiona retorted drily, lifting her cup to her mouth and setting it down again when she tasted the lukewarm bitterness of the tea.

'Is it? Fergus Mackay was your uncle, I know, but that never brought you all the way across the Atlantic before.' The speculative look turned to spitefulness. 'You think you're going to walk in here and take everything over, don't you? But you won't! Roderick's the one who's worked to build up Glenappon to what it is today, and Fergus Mackay looked upon him as a son. Do you think he would leave the estate to somebody he had never seen?'

'I don't see what business it is of yours,' Fiona contained her wrath with difficulty, 'but Glenappon can never belong to Roderick Cairns or anyone else. My father is the only remaining member of this branch of the Mackay family, and there's no question that Glenappon belongs to him.'

'That's not true! Glenappon belongs to Roderick, not to somebody who hasn't set foot in his homeland for years and years!'

Fiona looked across at the indignant glint in the other girl's eyes. 'I still don't see what Mackay family business has to do with you.'

'Don't you now! Well, it should interest you to know that Roderick and I are going to be married as soon as the proper period of mourning has passed.'

Fiona's gaze went from the dark passionate eyes to the full curve of the other girl's mouth. Could she be speaking the truth? Did Roderick Cairns really intend to marry her when the ripples caused by Fergus's death smoothed out again? It didn't seem likely, but then who was she to judge? Maybe that was how they did things over here ... an attractive girl who knew her way around the Highlands, whose roots were buried alongside those of a man almost destined by fate to become her husband.

'Congratulations!' she said drily, rising and skirting the table on her way to the door. Looking back from there, she added, 'But don't count on being mistress of Glenappon. My father, and I, come between Roderick Cairns and this estate.'

The younger girl followed her into the hall with its dust motes dancing in the errant shafts of sunlight.

'I don't care,' her voice echoed hollowly under the high, cavernous ceiling. 'Fergus Mackay knew that Roderick cared more for Glenappon than any upstart Americans! What do you know about old women who have spent their lives in service to the Mackays of Glenappon? Mary Anderson, the old woman he was supposed to go and see today—her whole existence was Glenappon Castle. She cared for Fergus Mackay when he was a child—aye, and your father, James. Tell me, Miss Mackay,' she called up to where Fiona had halted halfway up the stairs, 'did *you* ever hear of Rena Anderson?'

'No,' Fiona admitted, 'but you can bet your life that if my father knew her, she'll be one of the first he'll call on when he gets here in a day or two. Now if you'll excuse me, I'm going to my room to unpack.'

'You won't need to unpack very much,' the other girl sneered, her head swivelled at an upward angle so that she missed the entry from somewhere at the back of the hall of a formidable woman clad in sombre black. 'As the soon as the funeral's over, you'll be on your way back to America.'

'I'm thinking that will not be for you to decide,' a deep voice issued from the black bodice, and heavy jowls quivered disapprovingly. 'Away you go back to your father, girl, and see to his meal.'

Catriona glared venomously at the implacable figure, then let her blazing eyes rest on Fiona for a moment, but refrained from further comment as she stamped towards the impressive entrance to the castle. Fiona's eyes met the level stare of the woman below—presumably the 'Maggie' Isabel had seemed almost scared of—and she nodded and smiled tightly before moving on up the grand staircase to the privacy of her room.

God, she thought as she leaned back against the door, it was like an ancient melodrama! Darkbrowed hero and over-anxious girl-friend, grim but staunchly loyal housekeeper—the only problem was that she didn't feel herself to be the stricken heroine in a romantic novel. She had come here at her father's request, and would have no qualms about returning to the States when the time came.

Her suitcases had already been unpacked and her clothes hung neatly in the massive wardrobe, so she decided to spend Isabel's siesta time in investigating the castle and surrounds. The closed rooms surrounding her own revealed dimly-lit and sparsely furnished guest rooms which had obviously not been used for years. Her mind strayed again to her hotel idea ... it seemed criminal to have all this vacant space when tourists in search of ambience would pay highly for it. It would cost a fortune, of course, to bring the place tastefully up to modern standards, but. . . .

The last door she opened before the staircase was obviously occupied. This room was flooded with light and the double bed positioned between two windows bore evidence of having been made up recently. A man's hairbrushes were neatly arranged on a chest of drawers next to a wardrobe as vast as her own, and the tag end of a white linen handkerchief poking out from the first drawer of the chest indicated a hurried search inside it.

Hurried . . . this must be Roderick's room. If she needed confirmation, it was there in abundance. School pictures of what looked like football teams were hung at various levels and various stages of development round the room. Fiona's mouth automatically smiled in response to an impishly grinning twelve- or fourteen-year-old Roderick staring out at her from the fading pictures, sobering with him as later teenage years brought unsmiling reflections indicating the weight of maturity.

He looked so much nicer, she thought, her head on one side, when he smiled as he had that day in the car. Obviously he didn't agree with her, because every later picture portrayed him as serious in varying degrees. Except one.

This one was on the small, leather-topped desk between the remaining two windows. It showed Roderick as he must have been at twenty-two or three, laughing, his arm possessively lodged round the waist of a similarly laughing blonde girl. The background was tropical, white sand beach and towering palms. The blonde must be someone important to him if he kept her picture in constant view. The thought somehow irritated her. Why hadn't he married the girl if she was important to him? Now he was dallying with the affections of the young Catriona Baird, though she didn't believe the dark girl's assertion that they were going to be married.

Fiona glanced out of one of the windows and stepped towards it with an exclamation. This side of the room looked out on what must be Glenappon Loch, and it was breathtakingly beautiful. Majestic fir-clad mountains swept down to the small lake's farthest shores while smooth green hills undulated gracefully to yellow sand beaches closer to the castle. This was the lake, she thought sentimentally, where her father had fished as a boy, taking away lifetime memories of teeming trout and salmon. Not one boat marred the glittering smoothness of the loch's surface, so surely her father's coloured memories were just that.

But of course there wouldn't be any boats there, she realised with a tug of surprise. The loch, like so much of the surrounding countryside, belonged to the Mackay's of Glenappon . . . no one else could fish there without permission. It was an overwhelming thought. Her busy mind leapt ahead to advertising jargon . . . 'Private, well-stocked lake for the fisherman—try your skill with Highland trout and feisty Scotch salmon.'

The roar of a heavy-duty motor infiltrated her consciousness and she dashed instinctively to the other set of windows overlooking the courtyard. Roderick Cairns was getting out of the same vehicle he had used to transport her to Glenappon, and she stared thoughtfully as his dark head swooped into the rear of the vehicle and he re-emerged carrying a buff folder under his left arm.

As if aware of her scrutiny, he looked up and scanned the upper windows and Fiona shrank back into the room.

He couldn't have seen her, not through the distorting leaded glass, but she nevertheless beat a hasty retreat to the safety of her own room, leaning against the panels of its closed door and panting as if she had run a marathon race. She strained her ears for sounds of his entrance, but nothing filtered through the thick floors and walls. That must have been a drawback in the days of attack and intrigue, she reflected drily as she moved from the doorway into the room. The rug was sumptuously thick under her feet and she wondered irrelevantly if the blonde girl in that picture had occupied this room before her. Nocturnal visits by Roderick Cairns would have been equally undetectable.

'Will you have some more lamb?' Isabel Mackay offered, and Fiona declined with a strained smile. The evening meal, a close replica of lunch, followed 'tea' of sandwiches, cakes and cookies at four p.m. Admittedly it was now eight-thirty, but Fiona's stomach rebelled against such constant fortification. She was relieved, therefore, when the same maid who had served lunch came in and announced loudly,

'Miss Mackay is wanted on the telephone—I think it's from America,' she added in a less formal voice, letting her awe show through.

'Oh, that must be Dad.' Fiona hastily touched the white linen napkin to her mouth and leapt to her feet. 'Excuse me.'

The sombre black receiver in the alcove just outside the dining room was laid, off the hook, on top of a flower bedecked secrétaire. Fiona snatched it up and said breathlessly, 'Dad? I'm so glad to hear from you. . . .'

'Hey, it's not your father,' David's voice came amusedly over the line. 'It's me—David, remember?'

'David? Oh, hi, how are you?'

'Miserable without you. How long are you going to be away?'

'I'll be home as—well, I won't be away too long,' she amended carefully, conscious that her voice must be carrying easily through the open door of the dining room. 'How are you? Did you go to that party you thought would bore you out of your mind?'

'How wrong could I be?' his voice smiled complacently. 'It turned out that Janessa Fairbright has more than a little influence with her father. He's anxious to get into the hotel field—it's not surprising that he'd find that more interesting than churning out Y couplings, don't you think? Anyway, I don't think it will need much persuasion to get him interested in Mackay, Singapore. He has a lot of contacts in the Middle East and Asia, so there shouldn't be too much trouble in establishing Mackay Hotels there. How does Mackay, Singapore, sound to you?'

'Just fine,' Fiona returned abstractedly, at this moment more concerned with Glenappon Castle and its inhabitants. 'When is Dad coming over here?'

'To Scotland?' David made it sound like the ends of the earth. 'Let's see . . . he has to tie up the Florida deal, and then there's this Singapore thing—I'd say he'll be free in about four, five weeks.'

'Five weeks?' she repeated, aghast. 'He told me he'd be coming over here as soon as the Florida deal was complete.'

'Well, that's the way business goes, sweetie,' David commiserated ineffectually. She felt more alienated than ever from the ties that had bound her to the father she adored.

'Tell Dad,' she gritted, 'that he's needed here. I can't cope alone with,' she lowered her voice, 'the backbone of Scotland. Tell him to call me at the earliest possible time.'

David used his heavily official voice. 'I will as soon as I can get hold of him. I'm not exactly sure just where he is at this moment.'

In other words, James Mackay was spending a night or two with yet another woman he paid generously to substitute for the wife he had loved and lost. The only problem was that there wasn't enough money in the world to bring back the Eleanor of his happy earlier life.

'All right,' she agreed dully, letting the rest of David's conversation float unobtrusively over her. When there was a lengthy pause on the line, she added, 'Be sure to tell him when you talk with him that I need him here.'

'Honey, what's with you?' David came back unfeelingly at her ear. 'You sound desperate, and that's not like you. What does it matter about Glencarron, or whatever it's called? Your father has a lot more to think about than a hamlet in deepest Scotland. Hell, the whole of the Far East is opening up—do you really think James Mackay would let an opportunity like that go by?'

He was right. Fiona was letting the atmosphere of Glenappon get to her ... thick rock walls seemed to do something to her reasoning powers.

No dark bearded man was about to scoop her up on to his horse and gallop off into the night with her.

'And how was your father, dear?' Isabel enquired from the silence between her and her son. Either she was politely intimating that she hadn't deliberately eavesdropped, or she had a hearing problem.

Fiona slid back into her seat and took up her napkin again. 'It wasn't Dad, he's still busy on the deal he was negotiating in Florida. And I'm afraid he won't be coming as soon as I expected,' she went on, feeling no need to explain David or his call, 'because of another deal in Singapore.'

'My, what a busy life he leads,' Isabel murmured, 'he'll be glad of the break away from it all when he does come. I hope this news doesn't mean that you will be leaving us sooner?'

Fiona stared at her blankly. She was, after all, the daughter of the new Laird, and the question should more properly have been put by her to them. 'I can't decide that until I hear directly from Dad as to how long he'll be. David thought——' She paused, ridiculously feeling herself blushing furiously. 'It may be four or five weeks before he can make it,' she ended hurriedly.

'David?' Roderick blasted her hopes that her agitation hadn't been noticed. 'Is he your young man, then?'

At any other time, Fiona would have been vastly amused by the expression which was, by today's standards, archaic. Now she gave a glare in return to Roderick's levelly inquisitive stare.

'David is my father's Vice-president of Consumer Relations.'

His brows rose in mocking acknowledgment.

'An impressive title, but you didn't answer my question.'

'Roderick, stop badgering the girl,' his mother intervened, giving him a frowning look as she rose. 'I think it's time we went into the sitting room for our coffee.'

Fiona visualised the massive room she had blundered into earlier, but Isabel led the way into a much smaller one located next to the dining room. It was obviously the room most lived in, with its overstuffed and well-worn sofas and armchairs clustered cosily round a lit fireplace. Fiona gravitated at once to stand before this, holding her chilled hands out to its crackling blaze. This might be summer for Scotland, she shivered as warmth filtered through to her bones, but anywhere else in her world it would be considered a definitely cool March.

'You must miss the central heating,' Isabel noted her avid appreciation. 'Fergus wasn't one for newfangled notions. He always said that what had been good enough for his fathers was good enough for him.'

'That's easy to say,' her son said drily, dropping into what was evidently a familiar chair at one side of the fireplace, 'when he had fires going night and day, winter and summer, in any room he used.'

'That was only as he got older,' Isabel defended, seeming relieved when the sturdy maid brought in a silver tray laden with pots and bowls in similar heavy silver, and what seemed like a child's teaset for playing house. 'Thank you, Rena, I'll pour it myself.' She busied herself with the miniature cups as she went on, 'Now I know how you Americans love coffee, so I'll serve you yours first, Fiona. Will you take it black or white?'

'Er—white, please.' Fiona forced a smile as she accepted the dainty little cup and matching saucer. Something of her bewildered disappointment must have shown on her face, because Roderick spoke up from his chair with an amused drawl.

'Americans don't drink specially blended Turkish coffee, Mother, they buy it in bulk and drink it in outsized mugs. Isn't that right, Fiona?'

'We drink altogether too much coffee,' she compromised, unwilling to offend Isabel, who was so anxious to please.

'Oh dear,' the older woman frowned worriedly in her direction as she carried her son's coffee over to him, 'then you must let me know what coffee it is that you like. I don't care for it at all myself,' she confessed, 'it's much too strong and bitter for me.'

'I'll get some American coffee in—where do you do your shopping?'

'Most of our supplies come from the village shop,' Roderick volunteered caustically, 'and they're not likely to carry anything as exotic as American brands of coffee. I'll get some the next time I'm in Aberdeen, or Perth, or Edinburgh.'

The subject of coffee seemingly exhausted, a silence fell over them as they took small sips of the Turkish blend. Its acrid flavour determined Fiona to request tea the next time around.

'So,' Isabel broke the silence brightly, 'tell us about your life in America. You help your father in his business, I understand.'

'Yes—yes, I do.' Fiona placed her only half empty cup on a side table and took the armchair opposite Roderick's. 'I—well, I guess I mainly fill in for him in the area of——'

The phone rang in the hall and Isabel jumped up.

'I'll answer it, it's likely the Minister.'

Fiona glanced across at Roderick, who seemed supremely relaxed, his head wedged into the deeply winged chair. He had changed again for dinner, this time into, surprisingly, a formal business suit in dark grey worsted that emphasised his brooding good looks.

'Can I get you a liqueur to go with your coffee?'

'No—thanks. I seldom drink liqueurs ... in fact, I don't drink much of anything apart from white wine. The dinner wine was excellent.'

His head bowed in acknowledgment. 'I persuaded Fergus to lay in a few good bottles a year or two ago—though he himself, of course, never drank anything but the Scotch whisky that's made a few miles from here.'

Fiona looked at him curiously. 'Were you— close to him? I guess you must have been, since you lived here for so long.'

'I was as close as anyone could get to a man like Fergus,' he shrugged. 'I doubt if even his own son could have penetrated that crusty shell of his—but then you've heard from your father what Fergus was like.'

The only picture of Fergus that Fiona could conjure up was of his cold, stark profile looming up from that coffin in a room at the other end of the hall. A shiver ran over her. So far, Fergus Mackay hadn't been discussed in any detail. It was as if a king had died and everyone was too awed to speak his name in any human sense.

'Well now,' Isabel came back into the room mentally, if not physically, rubbing her hands together with satisfaction, 'everything is arranged. Hamish McIntyre,' she addressed her son exclusively, 'has agreed to act as one of the pallbearers after all. It's no more than he should do, of course,' she observed tartly, 'considering that Fergus stood up for him years ago when he was accused of selling his home-made whisky at a considerable reduction in price. Lady Carstairs has donated blooms from her greenhouses to decorate the church, and Tam Mackenzie has volunteered. . . .'

The words flowed over Fiona's consciousness. Heat from the redly glowing fire washed like a balm over her and her body relaxed in the deep seated chair. It was all so alien to her, so. . . .

Drowsy consciousness returned when she was lifted from the chair and carried in strongly tensed arms to the door. 'Uncle Fergus . . .' she struggled a little, 'oh, Dad, you should be here.'

'He'll be here,' she heard a far-off voice, and felt the delicious softness of a downy soft mattress under her. Fingers touched the front zipper of her midnight blue dress and she floated free of its confines as sleep overtook her again.

CHAPTER THREE

SHE could still feel the inexplicable smile that gently curved her mouth when full wakefulness came to her in the morning. As she stretched luxuriantly on the infinitely comfortable mattress, her eyes went up to the canopy overhanging her bed. Had Mary, Queen of Scots felt this relaxed four hundred years before when her lover, the Earl of Bothwell, had carried her off to his stronghold and wooed her so ardently that she had allowed him to become her third husband?

The comparison ended when, after a formal knock on the door, Rena approached the bed bearing the inevitable tray. Fiona panicked for a moment, having no recollection of undressing and donning her nightdress. Her fingers encountered the shoestring straps and she smiled as she returned the plump maid's greeting.

'Good morning. It seems to be a beautiful one.'

'Aye, it is that, miss. There's a mist on the loch yet, but it should have cleared by the time of the funeral.'

The comment sobered Fiona's carefree mood. How could she have forgotten that today was her Uncle Fergus's funeral?—that he still lay in solitary state in that vast room below? The question of just whose hands had undressed her faded into insignificance. She felt ashamed that she didn't even know the time of the funeral or where it would be held.

Rena deposited the tray firmly across her lap as she struggled to a sitting position, and she asked with seeming nonchalance, 'How much time do I have before the ceremony?'

The maid stared at her blankly. 'The——? Oh, you mean the funeral, miss. You've plenty of time, it's not till two o'clock this afternoon.' She looked hesitantly at Fiona. 'You'll pardon me, miss, but I noticed when I put your clothes away—well, I took you were not meaning to go to the funeral.'

It was Fiona's turn to stare. 'Why in the world not? That's the reason I came.'

'Do they not wear mourning clothes in America?' The thought evidently amazed Rena, and Fiona smiled her relief. The maid couldn't have noticed the royal blue skirt suit she had thoughtfully tucked into her suitcase as a last-minute thought.

'Women don't dress like witches any more, if that's what you mean.' Her smile faded. 'You mean they still do here, don't you?'

'Oh yes, miss. I don't know what would be said if you went to your uncle's funeral in ordinary clothes.' From Rena's distressed expression, Fiona could guess.

'Well, I don't carry widow's weeds with me, so they'll have to take me as I am.' Fiona lifted the teapot, amazed at how much she was looking forward to the strong tea after the vileness of the coffee last night.

'Oh, I don't think you'd better go at all if you haven't the right clothes for it.' Rena's distress intensified, irritating Fiona. The twentieth century had barely touched this remote settlement in the Highlands. It didn't help when Rena eyed her appraisingly and said doubtfully, 'I'll see if I can find somebody willing to lend you the proper clothes, although you're so slight I'm not sure——'

Not at all sure that she cared enough about ancient customs to the point of wearing an ex-widow's cast-offs, Fiona nevertheless appreciated Rena's concern. 'Thanks, but you really shouldn't bother. Everybody knows I'm an American and follow our own customs.'

'But you're also a Mackay of Glenappon, miss,' Rena reminded her, giving her food for thought long after the girl had hurried from the room.

The Mackay name *was* important here, more so in an insular way than in the international hotel world. As the new Laird's daughter, she would be expected to respect ancient customs. Damn! Why hadn't her father given her some inkling of what was expected of her? True, he had left Scotland as a young man, and couldn't be blamed for forgetting some of those customs—but what about Isabel? So far, she hadn't worn a thing that remotely resembled mourning clothes in the traditional sense. Her dress for dinner last night had been a soft shade of grey—which might suggest in its colourlessness a sign of respect for her dead husband.

As she ate sparsely from the gigantic breakfast that seemed a staple to start the day in Scotland, she wondered about her step-aunt. Had she loved Fergus Mackay, or had he just been a means to an end for her? Widowed, and with a young son to bring up, she must have been tempted to accept the first well-heeled man to come along. Though by all accounts, the Mackay fortunes had been on the downswing for quite some time. There was the worn stair and other carpets, the unused and uncomfortable rooms that had never been converted for guests ... all proof that money was in short supply. That wouldn't matter, she dismissed, when James Mackay took over as Laird. He had more than enough to restore Glenappon's grandeur and never miss it.

More to the point, what would Isabel Mackay and Roderick do now that their benefactor of years had passed on? Her father would see to it that Isabel was comfortably set up wherever she chose to go ... Roderick had a career he evidently preferred to the life of rural serenity.

Although, she thought later as she went past his room, he did seem to take an absorbing interest in Glenappon and its environs. He had hurried back from Edinburgh yesterday for the sole purpose of meeting with the—what was he?—the factor of the estate. It was he who made the decisions about spraying or not spraying the trees at the far side of the loch.

She found Isabel arranging flowers at the central table in the hall. Again, the older woman was dressed in non-mourning clothes. A pale pink blouse complemented a fine wool sweater in the same colour and a blue and pink tweed skirt.

'Good morning, Fiona,' she greeted brightly, making Fiona wonder again about how devastated the older woman was by her husband's death. 'I hope you slept well?'

'Very well. I didn't know a thing until Rena came in with my breakfast tray. And speaking of that,' she went on tactfully, her eyes on Isabel's quick fingers as they expertly arranged the flowers into blended height and colour, 'I'm really not used to that kind of luxury. In fact, I prefer to eat breakfast at a normal hour with everyone else.' She smiled into Isabel's quickly raised eyes. 'My day always starts early in New York or wherever I happen to be, and I don't think I can change that habit.'

'Well, of course, my dear. We want you to be comfortable and happy while you're here.' Giving the arrangement one more assessing look, Isabel took up the basket she had carried the flowers in from the garden and laid a friendly hand on Fiona's arm as they walked on down the hall. 'We just seem to be such a disorganised family at breakfast time. When Roderick's here, he's up and taken breakfast and out before I'm awake. He was born to be a forester, although his chosen career takes him far away from the hills and glens he loves so much.' She opened the door into the small sitting room they had used the night before. 'If you'll excuse me for a minute,

I'll go and get rid of this and see about some refreshment for us.'

Fiona wandered across to the windows on the east side, which overlooked the loch, as Roderick's room did above. A grizzle-haired man in denim overalls was mowing the lawn that led down to the narrow strip of sand beach bordering the loch. Mindlessly, she watched as he trod purposefully behind the concession to modern living, a gas-powered mower.

She didn't really care for more tea, even less for coffee, but the time she would spend with Isabel over it could prove invaluable in assuaging her curiosity on several points. The older woman showed no overt signs of grief over her husband's death. Moreover, she obviously expected to stay on at Glenappon as chatelaine. She must surely know that James Mackay was the only, the obvious, heir. Perhaps Isabel was one of those people who refused to face facts unpleasant to themselves until reality was forced on them. Her father, she knew, would never knowingly hurt another human being, and she could well imagine him inviting Isabel to stay on as long as she wished.

'Here we are,' the older woman bustled back into the room, herself bearing a tray which she set down on the low table in front of the empty fireplace. 'I'm afraid it's tea, until Roderick finds the kind of coffee you like.'

'Tea is fine.' Fiona sidestepped the chair Roderick had used the night before and took the one opposite, as she had then. 'Rena tells me that I have no clothes suitable for Uncle Fergus's funeral,' she opened the conversation. 'In America we don't lay too much stress on that kind of thing any more.'

She was surprised by her step-aunt's reaction. Isabel's hand visibly shook as she passed a brimming cup to Fiona and her eyes betrayed distress as they met the younger woman's.

'I'm afraid we do here,' she said agitatedly. 'I'm so sorry, Fiona, I didn't think to tell you. There are customs, you know. . . .'

It was a replay of Rena's conversation a short while ago, and Fiona felt the same irritation rising inside her. 'I hadn't realised,' she said shortly, her eyes going significantly over Isabel's non-mourning outfit, 'that black was *de rigeur* for an occasion like this.'

Isabel looked down at her pink and blue ensemble. 'Oh, you mean that I'm not presently dressed as a widow?' Her eyes held a deeply sad look as they lifted to Fiona's again. 'Fergus loathed widowed women to look like scarecrows, as he called them. Making themselves drab, he used to say, wouldn't bring a dead man back to life, but it could spoil the widow's chances of making a new match for herself. Not,' she added hastily, 'that I expect or want another husband. I'm just respecting Fergus's wishes when I wear other colours than black.'

'Yet you're going to wear it for the funeral?'

'Of course,' Isabel returned with dignity. 'It's expected, you see.' Then, as if sensing Fiona's acid incredulity, she added quietly, 'I loved Fergus Mackay, Fiona, don't doubt that. Not in the romantic sense of today, but for his good qualities that have little meaning now. Not many men would take on an impoverished widow with a young son, but Fergus did, and he gave meaning back to my life. I was in love in a romantic way with my first husband, Roderick's father, but I soon realised that while he was lovable had none of the stability a woman needs in the man she loves. He died not long after Roderick was born and I was left alone to bring him up as best I could. Fergus came one day to the small millinery shop I had started in desperation—he was looking for a gift for his wife,' she smiled nostalgically, 'and I had no idea that within six months his wife would be dead and I would be the new focus of his affection. Though,' her smile deepend, 'I think it was Roderick he cared for more than me. He had no children of his own, and Roderick was a beautiful boy. But I married Fergus,' she lifted her head proudly, 'because I cared for him. He was a man difficult to understand, but I think I did. All his life people had expected things of him ... his father first of all, who held Glenappon sacred. How Fergus would have loved, like your father, to test his wings in other fields! But that was denied to him, and he spent his life preserving the heritage handed down to him. He was a fine man in many ways, and I respected him for all he stood for.'

'Cared for him,' 'respected him,' were the phrases Isabel used. Nothing in her words or attitude suggested that she had loved Fergus Mackay with a woman's vibrant passion. Perhaps it had been enough for Isabel that the son of the man she had loved in that way would know the security of belonging, however spurious that security might be.

'Excuse me, madam,' Rena's tentative voice penetrated Fiona's abstracted soliloquy, 'I think I've found the clothes Miss Mackay will be needing for the funeral. You'll recall that Mrs

Petrie lost her husband last year, and as she is about the same size as Miss Mackay, I thought——'

'Yes, indeed,' Isabel brightened, her eyes sweeping across Fiona's slender figure in soft blue polyester pants suit. 'The size should match perfectly.'

That the subject was grossly distasteful to Fiona seemed not to occur to Isabel Mackay or the maid, but Fiona herself felt a deep revulsion at the thought of wearing the weeds of last year's widow. She had never worn the cast-off clothes of anyone, let alone those of a recently bereaved woman, but Isabel seemed to see nothing wrong in the arrangement.

'Oh, that's good,' she approved, her eyes going over Fiona's tautly slim figure, much as Rena's had earlier. 'Yes, the clothes should fit her, though it doesn't matter if they're a little loose. Well done, Rena,' she ended with a smile to the maid.

'I really don't think I——' Fiona began, only to be squashed by the Scottish maid's voluble overriding of her softly spoken protest.

'Mrs Petrie has promised to bring the clothes to the castle by one o'clock. That will give Miss Mackay plenty of time to dress before the funeral.'

'Yes—thank you, Rena.' Isabel's voice held a quiet command that Fiona envied when she saw the results. The maid said no more, withdrawing quietly to the door and closing it after her.

'Isabel, I really don't——' Fiona began.

'Of course you don't,' the older woman said tranquilly, 'but for the family's sake, I'm sure you will forgo any distaste you might feel about wearing Marianne Petrie's clothing. I can assure you that it will be scrupulously clean. Mrs Petrie is meticulous about her dress, and she would be particularly careful of clothes intended to be worn by . . . by you.'

By the new Laird's daughter? The thought involuntarily entered Fiona's mind but remained unsaid. 'It's not that,' she said awkwardly, 'it's just that . . . well, this is all very strange to me. I've been to few funerals, and only as an absolute outsider.'

'Yes, I know it must be strange to you,' Isabel returned comfortably, 'but Fergus would have expected his niece to do the right thing.'

The right thing, Fiona decided a few hours later as she surveyed herself in the dresser mirror, might be fine for Fergus Mackay, but it would do nothing for her image as an up-and-coming executive in her father's hotel empire.

The dress Rena had borrowed from the widow Petrie fitted the contours of her figure but reached just below calf-length, giving her the look of a Thirties matron. She was too embarrassed to note that her bright red-gold hair contrasted stunningly with the stark black of the dress, and that she looked more startlingly beautiful than she had in her life before.

'I positively cannot wear this,' she announced dramatically to a hovering Rena. 'I look like something out of a Sir Walter Scott tragedy!'

'Oh no, miss, you look very nice. The Laird would be proud of you if he could see you.' Rena crossed to the window when the sounds of yet another vehicle rose from the castle entrance below. 'It's Lady Carstairs!' she said excitedly, turning back to chivvy Fiona into action. 'Be quick, miss, you should be down in the hall to greet her.'

Fiona's first impulse was to retort that she wouldn't greet the devil himself in such a garb, but the whole thing obviously meant so much to Rena, and consequently to the inhabitants of Glenappon, that she curbed her tongue. What would it hurt, she shrugged mentally, to go through with this masquerade? David would roar with laughter if he could see her ... but he wouldn't see her.

She walked in the unfamiliar clothes to the head of the stairs and paused there, looking down on the scene below. Isabel was scarcely recognisable in deep mourning, a close-meshed veil similar to the one Fiona had tossed back from her own head lowered over her features, obscuring them. Catriona Baird, her stocky figure slimmed by a black dress, talked with unseemly animation to the man bent politely over her. Roderick.

Fiona took in his appearance in one swift glance ... a study in black, the white exposure of shirt at his chest and neck contrasted sharply with his dark colouring. An alien rush of feeling swept over her when his firm mouth parted in a white-toothed smile for Catriona's benefit. Whether or not he was engaged to the black-haired girl, this was surely no time for casual badinage. Particularly as solemn-looking men were disappearing into the room where Fergus Mackay lay for the last few minutes of his time under the roof he had never left in his life.

Roderick looked up and saw her, his face sobering as his head tilted back. All Fiona's uncertainty must have been in her eyes, and he left Catriona's side immediately to come to the bottom of the staircase, leaving the dark girl talking to the air where he had been. Her head, like everyone else's when Roderick moved across the hall, turned to look up at the frozen Fiona.

Ridiculous as it seemed, considering her background, she was incapable of movement until Roderick leapt lightly up the stairs and drew her trembling arm through his.

'Why are they all staring at me like that?' she whispered fiercely, her fingers curving round the hard muscled forearm. It helped even more when he laid his free hand over hers and pressed it.

'I doubt if they've ever seen anyone as beautiful as you at Glenappon,' he murmured back as they started down the stairs, 'and you're unmistakably a Mackay, with that red hair and blue eyes. They're also curious because you never came while Fergus was alive.'

Curious? Or hostile? The question slid to the back of her mind as the sea of faces became individual ones which Roderick briefly introduced her to and whose names she vainly tried to remember ... the regal, full-figured matron with white hair piled on top of her head under black veiled hat was Lady Carstairs ... the tall, thin, stooped and lugubrious-looking man who might have been the undertaker turned out to be Henry McAlpine from Aberdeen, her uncle's lawyer .. several ruddy-faced men who were apparently the farmers of Glenappon estate all seemed to have names that began with 'Mac' and Fiona decided to sort them out later ... a hefty younger man with sandy hair and pale blue eyes framed with almost invisible lashes was Craig Jameson, the factor.

'Roderick, you're needed in there now,' Isabel laid a black gloved hand on his arm and nodded towards the room where the husky farm men had emerged from and had now re-entered.

Until he left her with one last squeeze on the hand that had never left his arm Fiona hadn't realised just how much she had been leaning on his support, mental and physical. As his well-set shoulders disappeared through the doorway she felt bereft. Those whose eyes she met looked away immediately and studied the floor with absorbed interest . . . except for Catriona, who stared at her with unconcealed venom. Fiona was glad when there was movement towards the door and a falling back to either side of it when the coffin, borne on six broad shoulders with Roderick's at the front end, passed through to the waiting vehicle. Another ancient Rolls carried herself and Isabel down the hill to the village and through it, turning off on a small side road to a grey stone church nestled among towering trees and massive flowering shrubs.

Fergus had reached his last resting place.

'It's a great pity, Miss Mackay, that you didn't meet your uncle in his lifetime,' the Reverend John Russell, middle-aged, thin, and bespectacled, voiced the thought—censure—Fiona felt emanating from every member of the gathering for Fergus's funeral. That, seemingly, encompassed not only the villagers and workers connected with the estate, but the entire surrounding area.

She was rapidly becoming defensively irritated by the mainly unspoken criticism, and her voice was cool when she answered the Minister who stared at her owlishly from behind his thick-lensed glasses.

'I think my uncle understood how difficult it was

for my father or me to make such a long journey, with so many other demands on our time.'

'Oh yes,' he gazed at the dining room ceiling as if his memories were inscribed there, 'I believe your father, James Mackay, is in the hotel business.' He made it sound as if her father ran a chain of sleazy one-night stopovers. 'Does he not have one in London?'

'Yes.'

A pained smile touched his narrow mouth. 'That's not so far away from his homeland, he could surely have taken a day or two to visit his brother.'

Two red spots of anger dotted Fiona's cheeks. 'It must be difficult for a country clergyman to understand the pressure of business life, Mr— Russell?' she flared. 'My father planned a visit home for many years, but he wouldn't have insulted his family by snatching a one- or two-day visit when he could spare the time. He loved this place so much that he brought me up on stories about it, and I loved it too and recognised it when I came. Would my father think about retiring here if he——?'

'Fiona, there's somebody here who would like to meet you,' Roderick intervened smoothly from behind her shoulder, putting a firm hand on her elbow and smiling at the older man. 'Excuse us, Minister.'

They had crossed the dining room and emerged into the hall when Fiona took a deep breath and expelled it explosively. 'Look, I don't think I can take any more hostility today.' She shook her head. 'I really thought the people here would be glad to see me, to welcome the last of the Mackays of Glenappon, but they all seem to hate me.'

'They don't hate you.' Roderick walked her across the hall and opened a solid door she hadn't noticed before under the curve of the staircase, ushering her into a small room set up as an office. A man's office, replete with ancient desk and battered black leather chairs and sofa and faded prints of sombre Highland scenes spaced round the oak-panelled walls. The room was empty.

'I thought you said——' she swung round enquiringly.

'I guessed you were near the end of your tether,' he said matter of factly, indicating the sofa along one wall and walking to a small cabinet beside the tiled fireplace. 'I'm going to pour you some whisky and you're going to drink it. Even at the best of times, if such a thing is possible, a funeral can be a stressful experience.'

'You'd never know it,' Fiona retorted bitterly, dropping into one corner of the sofa and removing the headdress that had annoyed her ever since she had put it on. 'Is a Scottish funeral always like this? It's more like a party than anything . . . I've never seen so much food disappear so fast!'

Roderick turned, smiling as he came over and handed her one of the two glasses in his hands. 'It's the custom, something like an Irish wake, though I hope this one won't go on as long as that.' He took the leather armchair at right angles to where she sat. 'It's not that they're uncaring.'

'You could have fooled me,' she said drily. 'Why, even Isabel——' She stopped and bit softly on her underlip. What a time to forget that Isabel was his mother!

'You think my mother is uncaring?' he asked quietly, his eyes on the rich gold liquid in his glass. 'I assure you she is not. Since his death, she has spent the biggest part of every night sitting beside him, as she did during his last long illness. No, Fiona,' he looked up with intent but not angry eyes, 'she isn't uncaring, she's just thankful that he's free of pain and at peace.'

Embarrassment rose in a painful wash over her neck and face. How tactless could a person be?—and mistaken! 'I—I'm sorry, Roderick, I didn't know that, and I shouldn't have made snap judgments on people I hardly know.'

He smiled wryly. 'Am I to presume you made a similar kind of judgment on me?'

'No, I——' she protested, then decided on honesty. 'Yes, I did,' she confessed. 'No one seemed to really care for Fergus himself. There was almost a—a joyful feeling about the place. Even today——' she paused and took a bracing mouthful of the pungent whisky, 'when I came down I saw you laughing with Catriona as if you were going to a garden party, not a funeral!'

He shrugged. 'The same reason applies. Fergus himself would have been the first one to celebrate a happy release from a world he no longer cared to inhabit.'

'Of course, I know that it's different when a man laughs with his future wife, even at a funeral,' she pursued—probed?—'but even so——'

Had she really cared, Roderick's reaction would have thrilled her completely.

'My *what*?'

'Well, Catriona mentioned——'

'Whatever she mentioned,' he cut in brusquely, 'I have never asked her to be my wife. There's never been any suggestion that such a thing would happen. No, Fiona, I have another woman entirely in mind to fill that position.'

He made it sound like an open competition for a
typist in his office, and Fiona felt a wild rise of
hysteria in her throat, aided, she admitted, by the
unaccustomed rise of dizzying fumes from the
whisky to her brain. 'Dear Sir,' flashed before her
eyes, 'I would like to apply for the position of your
wife, and my qualifications are:—'

A more sober memory of the picture in his
bedroom recalled the laughing blonde girl on a
tropical beach. He must mean her.

'Congratulations!' She had to force the word
and its accompanying smile—what was wrong
with her? It had to be the whisky hitting an empty
stomach . . . she hadn't eaten since that toyed-with
gargantuan breakfast this morning.

'I don't think you understand what I mean.' In
an instant, Roderick had transferred his glass to a
side table and his infinitely attractive body to the
cushion next to hers on the sofa. 'Fiona, I'm
asking you to be my wife.'

What remained of her drink swayed dangerously
in the glass and he took it from her, leaning across
her to place it beside his, one arm stretched along
her shoulders that stayed in place when he only
partially drew back. Fiona drew and expelled an
unsteady breath.

'I think this drink is making me hear things,' she
said faintly, although her strong awareness of his
male scent had nothing to do with whisky fumes.

'No, it's true, I want to marry you. From the
first minute I saw you in the arrival lounge at
Edinburgh Airport I knew that you were the
woman I'd waited for all this time.' His hand slid
under her jaw and brought her face round to his
darkly gleaming eyes. 'I know you're going to say
we hardly know each other, but it's as if I've

known you all my life. That first night in the hotel, I lay awake just watching you sleep. It seemed so—so right that we should be there together.'

The surprising thing, she thought much, much later, was that his words made beautiful sense at the time. It was like the unfolding of one of her father's fantasy tales about dark, mysterious Scotland, the ones that always had a satisfying ending. The princess, in this case herself, married the commoner who was immediately transformed into the prince who ruled their joint kingdom.

'Roderick, you're being foolish,' she summoned up the turn-down that had been effective a dozen times before. 'We *do* hardly know each other. . . .'

The remembered speech would have gone on to make it subtly clear that she was aware of the primary reason for the romantic interest. Namely, that she was James Mackay's only child, the heir to his vast kingdom. This time it was different . . . she had always been coolly level-headed in coping with male passion, but Roderick Cairns had a style all his own. Whether from instinct or experience, he knew just exactly the points of her pleasure.

His mouth came down warm and hard on hers, stifling her objections with the mastery of lips that made a fine art of kissing. He seemed to create a world inhabited solely by the two of them, with himself as skilled master. He brought forcibly to her attention how unskilled she was in coping with a man's determined passion . . . she could parry the forceful thrust of his lips over her own, but she was helpless against the provocative caress of his hands at breast and hip and thigh.

Insulated as they were from sounds from the rest of the house, there was only the snatch of hurried breathing, the unreal softness of her moans as she mindlessly responded to the abrasively intent sweep of his roving fingers.

'Roderick?' she breathed in a half-question, her own fingers hesitant as they touched and passed over the taut lines of his flat hips, gaining strength and power as they dealt feverishly with the buttons of his white shirt and slid under the narrow opening to the damp warmth of his hair-covered chest.

Her fingers tensed, her fingernails digging in what must have been painful fashion when the door was thrown open and a chorus of stridently alcoholic voices flooded into the room.

'Oh, this is where you are!' Isabel's relieved yet censorious voice reached them.

'Mother. . . .' Roderick got to his feet with remarkable aplomb, drawing Fiona up with him and at the same time re-fastening the gaping buttons of his shirt, 'Fiona has consented to be my wife.'

Isabel's eyes went caustically from one dishevelled figure to the other. 'I would certainly hope so, though I think now is not the time to announce a wedding. Some of our guests are leaving, Roderick, and they have been wondering where you had got to.'

'Isabel, I——' Fiona began, hot waves of embarrassment prickling across her skin, 'this isn't what it seems.'

'I would hope for your sake that it is what it seems,' Isabel retorted coldly. 'Roderick, you go on and bid farewell and—Fiona and I will follow shortly.'

He seemed about to say something more, then he shrugged almost imperceptibly and went out. Isabel remained silently just inside the door he closed behind him.

'Isabel,' Fiona started forward, realising how distasteful the scene of passion she had walked in on must seem to the newly bereaved widow, 'I'd really like to explain how all this happened,' she gestured unhappily towards the black leather sofa. 'Roderick brought me in here to——'

'I see perfectly well what my son brought you in here for,' Isabel said shortly, her eyes stoically fixed on the mid-section of the staunch wooden door. 'I think it would not be in the best of taste to announce your marriage for at least a month. We owe that much respect to Fergus.'

'There was no intention of——' Fiona began hotly, her ire cooling as she glanced down at the stark black of Mrs Mackay's mourning clothes. It *had* been disrespectful to Fergus's memory to make passionate love, dressed like this, to his stepson on the very day of his funeral. She felt boxed-in suddenly, as if outside forces were taking control of her life. The words that would have denied any intention of marrying Roderick, a virtual stranger, died in her throat. How could she add further to the anguish of this, if Roderick was to be believed, devoted widow in her hour of trial?

'When you are ready,' Isabel looked pointedly at the abandoned hat and veil, 'we'll go out and say goodbye. Later, we can talk about—all this.'

Fiona, after only a brief hesitation when she re-donned the hated headgear, followed the older woman into the hall feeling like a child who had behaved badly at a party. In Isabel's eyes, she reflected as she smiled automatically and shook the hands of departing guests, she supposed she had behaved badly. However much she blamed Roderick for initiating the scene, she still had to face the fact that she had put up little, if any, resistance.

Not until later, when she could escape to her room to change from the hideous clothes, did the thought that had been circulating at the back of her mind surface for inspection.

Isabel might have been shocked at coming upon such a scene on the day of her husband's funeral, but she hadn't been at all surprised by her son's announcement.

CHAPTER FOUR

By the time Fiona had changed into a simple dark brown skirt and chocolate-coloured sweater and walked down the stairs again, the certainties seething in her mind had sent bright red flags into her cheeks.

Roderick and his mother must think her a brainless idiot if they thought she couldn't see how they were trying to use her. What could be more comfortable all around if the displaced stepson married the heiress to not only Glenappon, but the huge Mackay Hotels empire? The estate could be restored to its one-time grandeur, and Roderick would one day be its master. His 'chosen profession' as he called it would very quickly lose its appeal if he was in command at Glenappon, which he admittedly loved. As for Isabel ... nothing would really change for her, she wouldn't be shunted off to some impecunious existence as she had been on the death of her first husband.

She was surprised to see, when she entered the small sitting room, that Henry McAlpine, her uncle's lawyer, hadn't left with the others but sat comfortably in an armchair sipping the tea Isabel was dispensing from the tray on a side table.

'Ah, here you are, Fiona,' the older woman greeted her warmly, 'will you take some tea?'

About to refuse, Fiona changed her mind. What she had to say was the stuff dry mouths were made of. Nodding acceptance, she ignored Roderick's obvious expectation that she would join him on the deep cushioned sofa facing the fire and went over to a side chair removed slightly from the grouping. Roderick hesitated before resuming his seat, a puzzled frown dimming the deep-seated gleam in his dark eyes. And why wouldn't he have a gleam in his eyes, she mocked silently as she smoothed her skirt and crossed her knees to stop their trembling. His world was turning out rosy, rosy all the way. He thought.

'Mrs Mackay has kindly asked me to stay overnight,' Henry McAlpine divulged, his sallow cheeks still flushed from the funeral liquor he had imbibed. 'It seemed unnecessary for me to go all the way back to Aberdeen and make the journey again for the reading of your uncle's will. It's a very simple document, so it won't entail much time tomorrow morning.'

Fiona was surprised to hear that her uncle had made a will. Everything must be quite straight-forward in a case of this kind, although she supposed Fergus had wanted to make small bequests to servants and estate workers who had served him faithfully through the years. Isabel, too, she recognised, was probably a major beneficiary as far as the impoverished estate went.

'I'm sure that my father, when he gets here,' she said coolly, 'will be happy to supplement my uncle's wishes. Glenappon and it's people are still

very close to his heart, and he's a generous man.'
Her eyes were frosty as they met first Roderick's,
then Isabel's almost identical dark eyes.

'Well,' Henry McAlpine cleared his throat in the
silence that followed her words, 'I am sure that
Roderick will be very pleased to take any help
offered for the upkeep of Glenappon, which as
you must know, is considerable in these days of
high wages and exorbitant prices. My wife——' he
digressed, but Fiona heard nothing of his
dissertation on the price of household necessities.

Was she crazy, or had she heard him say that
Roderick would be pleased to accept help to run
Glenappon? Glenappon was nothing to do with
Roderick, except in the most tenuous sense, yet the
lawyer was sounding as if he, and not James
Mackay, was the heir to this remote kingdom. The
lawyer must be more befuddled than she suspec-
ted.

'Fortunately,' she cut into the lawyer's dissertation, 'my father has the means to restore
Glenappon to the way it was meant to be.
Without,' she turned cold blue eyes on Roderick,
'the help of Mr Cairns.'

The silence that followed her words was deeper
than any she had ever known. Her eyes lingered
longest on Roderick's, where one emotion after
another chased across them. Surprise, embarrassment, *pity*. She looked quickly at Isabel and
then the lawyer, and found the same emotions
reflected there.

'I don't understand,' she said faintly, and Henry
McAlpine cleared his throat again.

'Your uncle has made it clear,' his voice
emphasised embarrassment 'that as Roderick is
more closely connected to Glenappon and its

affairs he should rightly—er—remain here and devote his life to it. Fergus made no secret of that part of his will,' he said apologetically.

'He certainly did!' Fiona flared hotly. 'My father expected, quite rightly, that Glenappon would be his, as the last of the Mackay men. It's——' she waved a jerky hand, 'an automatic thing.'

'Fiona. . . .' Roderick began, getting up and coming to stand over her.

'In this case,' the lawyer still sounded apologetic, 'that is not so. You must remember that your father, James Mackay, has displayed no interest in the welfare of Glenappon since he left it. Fergus devoted his life to it, and naturally wanted someone who felt the same to take over from him. I'm afraid, my dear, that when your father quarrelled with him and left Scotland, making no attempt at reconciliation in all these years, he assumed James had no interest in his inheritance.'

Fiona stared at him blankly, scarcely feeling the hard warm touch of Roderick's hand on her shoulder. A thousand thoughts flitted through her head . . . her father had talked about—and postponed!—so many visits to his homeland over the years. He had always made it seem as if the pressures of business kept him away. Never once had he mentioned to her a quarrel with his elder brother. Even now, for that brother's funeral, he had made excuses not to attend it.

Excuses . . . they hadn't seemed like that when he had voiced them. The Florida deal *was* important . . . the Singapore Mackay *was* an added feather in the Mackay chain bonnet. . . . Oh no, she thought sickly, had he ever really intended to come to Glenappon, or would there always be another Florida, another Singapore to detain him? Had he sent her, as he sometimes did on lesser deals, to represent him in the takeover of Glenappon?—a place that held nostalgic memories and little else for him? No, that couldn't be so. He loved this place so ... so much that he had transferred his feelings deliberately to his daughter. He would never give it up, not to a usurper like Roderick Cairns, unconnected by blood to the Mackays.

It felt as if the silence of her thoughts had taken minutes, but she supposed dully, when Roderick spoke at last, that only seconds had passed.

'Fiona, I thought you must know that Fergus had this in mind.' He knelt beside her chair in what, in different circumstances, would have seemed a theatrical gesture, but Fiona was too dumb to make the judgment. 'That was stupid of me, because I knew there had been no communication between the brothers for many years. They quarrelled,' he said earnestly, ignoring the presence of the others, 'because your father wanted to go and leave Glenappon when old Angus Mackay died.'

Of course, Fiona accepted dully. James Mackay didn't have it in him to play second fiddle to any man, least of all the older brother who had inherited lock, stock and barrel the home he loved. That, she realised now, had been the impetus that had driven him to found the Mackay chain ... to hell with you, he had said figuratively to the brother he held in awe, look what I can do.

'I have to call Dad,' she said faintly, oblivious of Roderick's consoling hands falling away from her as she rose and walked woodenly towards the door. She had to hear it from his own lips that when his spur to fame had died James Mackay no longer cared about his Scottish heritage.

Her voice was remote as she placed the call to the New York offices of Mackay Hotels.

'If you'll replace your receiver,' the operator told her in a precise, strongly accented voice, 'I'll call you back.'

Fiona leaned against the wall, numbness giving way to her more normal grasp on reality as moments ticked by. Projecting herself ahead to New York time, she realised that it was now after ten p.m. there. The Mackay offices would have been closed for hours. She should have called her father's apartment. Her hand was on the black receiver when it rang threadily.

David's clipped voice mingled with the operator's. 'Hello? Fiona? I was just about to call you ... dammit, you'd think the newsmen would give a little leeway before busting out with the news!'

'News?' she questioned vaguely, then presumed he was referring to the newest Mackay acquisition in Singapore. 'Listen, David, I want to talk to Dad. I'd forgotten about the time change, but I guess I'll get him at his apartment.'

She thought he said, 'Oh, my love,' but the line was far from clear. 'I have to talk to him, David, it's really vital. Has he gone to Singapore yet?'

This time there was no mistake. 'Oh, love,' David said clearly, 'you mean you don't know?'

'Know what?' she responded irritably. At that moment, the fate of Mackay, Singapore, meant less to her than the crisis surrounding her at Glenappon. 'I'll call the apartment,' she said, frustrated, wondering if David, after all, was as level headed as her father took him to be.

'No, don't do that. Fiona, I don't know how to tell you this——' he sounded hopelessly out of his depth, 'but your father's had a—a heart attack.'

Fiona's fingers froze clammily round the receiver. 'A—a heart attack?' she faltered. A great gulf yawned in her mind. 'How bad is it? I—I'll come right away.'

'Fiona, it was—really bad,' David's voice seemed to come from a distant planet. 'He—didn't make it, Fiona.'

Make it? Of course James Mackay had made it, whatever 'it' was. There wasn't a challenge in the world that he wouldn't face and conquer, even——

'Is he dead?' she asked starkly, and found the telephone wrenched abruptly from her hand. But even as she reeled back and sought the solidity of the wall behind her, she knew that her dynamic father had succumbed to the one will greater than his own. It would take that to demolish James Mackay . . . irrelevantly, she felt thankful that he had been spared the knowledge that his brother had disinherited him at the last. She watched like an impartial observer while Roderick, his shoulders hunched and his back to her, completed the conversation with David. Curiously detached, she weighed one man against the other and found it odd that they seemed to have so much to talk about . . . they were complete opposites. David was New York business born and bred, while Roderick possessed all the mystical charms of her father's homeland.

Tears were running unchecked down her cheeks when at last Roderick put down the phone and turned back to her, his face ashen. Saying nothing, he gathered her against his tweed-smelling chest and just held her, while the effortless tears soaked the fresh white of his shirt front.

'I think when you get through to your father,'

Henry McAlpine's soft voice came from behind them, 'you should tell him that——'

'For pity's sake, man!' Roderick's irritated rasp echoed in her ear, 'her father is dead. Leave us.'

'Oh dear heaven,' Isabel said faintly in the background.

'The same applies to you, Mother. Just leave us for a while.'

His voice murmured softly as he led Fiona across the hall and into the intimate smallness of the office where he had made love to her so recently. The words didn't penetrate Fiona's numbed consciousness, however, until he seated her in the same position at one edge of the couch.

'Your father was more successful than any other man in this part of Scotland. You owe it to him, as his daughter, to show what the Mackays of Glenappon are made of.'

What were they made of? Elusive memories her father had never dared put to the test.

'I have to go back,' she said faintly.

'Will you remember that I've asked you to be my wife?' Roderick asked tensely, his eloquent hands subdued as they softly caressed the soft flesh of her shoulders, evoking fleeting memories of her reactions to his touch a few hours ago. Now she could feel nothing.

'I have to go back,' she repeated tonelessly. More immediate than the physical comfort Roderick could provide was the stark reality of yet another funeral, one more poignantly real than the uncle's whom she had never seen. This was her father, the man who had been the touchstone of her existence since her beginning . . . .

'Do you feel up to talking to some reporters?'

David asked solicitously six days later, the trauma of her father's funeral only three days behind her. 'They're anxious to know if you'll be making any noticeable changes to the Mackay dynasty.'

'No, there won't be any changes,' she told him in the same level tone she had assumed since her return. 'You can tell them that Mackay Hotels will run as smoothly as they ever did, thanks to the management set-up my father initiated.'

David's fine-featured face seemed blurred suddenly.

'Fiona, you seem so different since you went over to Scotland,' he complained in a hard voice that softened as he went on, 'You know your father relied on me a lot, honey. There's nothing he'd want more than to know that you had someone at your side who cares about Mackay . . . and you, of course,' he tacked on hastily. 'Why don't we get married, and you can leave the business details to me?'

It wasn't the most romantic proposal she had received—that honour went to Roderick Cairns who, knowing she was about to make a gigantic fool of herself, had gone ahead anyway. Of course, even he hadn't been completely immune from the lure of Mackay money. Glenappon would flourish with it, die without it. As his wife, Fiona would be eminently suitable for his purposes. Unlimited funds would flow from a doting wife motivated by sentimental ties to her father's homeland.

'I'm too busy to think about marriage right now,' she told David brusquely, emphasising her point as she drew a pile of correspondence towards her. The desk was her father's, the responsibility was now hers. 'Ask Carol to come in on your way out, will you?' she asked levelly, pleasantly. 'Oh, and set up a meeting with the Mazzini Brothers about the property in Sicily ... I'm free on the. . . .' she rifled through the desk diary, 'twentieth of this month. Let's make it a morning meeting.'

David lingered until she looked up irritably to ask, 'Is there something else?'

'No,' he said slowly, 'there's nothing else.'

Her façade collapsed as soon as he went through the door to the outer office, closing it behind him. Oh, Dad, she silently implored, why did you leave me with all this?

Not just the overwhelming responsibility of making the decisions for a vast corporate enterprise, she thought bleakly as she rose and looked down at the ant-like crawl of traffic below. He had left her a heritage much more tortuous emotionally. Glenappon and all it stood for.

Two years could go amazingly fast when the business world pressed its demands and excluded the everyday affairs of the world. The worst recession in years affected the hotel industry as much as any other; companies jealously tightened purse strings on funds that would normally be spent on conventions; the Mackay chain, like other hotels, suffered the consequences.

Fiona felt herself visibly age under the constant stress, although, she decided as she prepared for an evening sponsored by the Travel Agents of America, she looked crisply self-assured in a short evening dress of black silk that contrasted strikingly with her bright red-gold hair and smooth white shoulders.

She had moved into her father's more spacious apartment shortly after his death, but the huge master bedroom had scarcely changed. There were no feminine touches to relieve its starkly utilitarian lines, and the rest of the apartment followed suit. The spacious living room with its adjoining patio overlooking Central Park was still furnished in her father's taste. Off-white broadloom lent distinction to the stark lines of Scandinavian furniture and contrasted with the priceless paintings brought into prominence on the white-painted walls by individual spotlights that sprang to life whenever the main switches were turned on. The only exotic accent in the apartment was the maid, Carlotta's, light brown skin.

'Will you be needing me tonight?' Carlotta questioned as she walked through from bedroom to living room. 'My brother's coming back from a year in Guatemala, and I'd like to be there for the celebration.'

'That's fine,' Fiona agreed abstractedly, her mind intent on the speech she would deliver to the combined forces of the travel business later that evening. 'Enjoy yourself,' she called after the speedily departing Carlotta, knowing the other woman would consider her crazy if she confessed her own loneliness.

It wasn't loneliness for casual acquaintances, she thought wistfully as she crossed to the bar and poured herself a pre-dinner drink of white wine over ice cubes. Carlotta had a family, knit closely to one another, while she. . . .

The doorbell buzzed, and she waited for Carlotta to answer it. When it repeated its low-toned burr, she realised that the maid had already left and she set her drink down on the hall bureau as she went to answer it.

Blurred, unrecognisable features reflected back

through the peephole she automatically peered through, and she took the precaution of fastening the chain lock before opening the door sufficient inches to give her a clear view of the caller.

'Fiona?' a male voice asked, and her mouth ran suddenly dry. No other man said her name in just that way, and yet. . . .

'Roderick?' she breathed, disbelieving.

'Yes. I wondered if I might speak to you for a few minutes.'

'Of course,' she said, her mind a mass of confusions. What was he doing here in New York so far from Glenappon? Not, she noted as he brushed past her, that he wanted to boost his fortunes from Mackay Hotels. He looked prosperous, though somewhat heavily dressed for New York's August heat in a grey tweed suit. His dark-jawed face was thinner than she remembered, his eyes more snappily alert as they appraised the high-ceilinged entrance hall with its carefully placed alcoves to accommodate the statuary her father had collected.

'It's a very nice place you have here,' he commented in the accent she had foolishly thought she had forgotten. Over a sudden lump in her throat, she said strainedly,

'It was my father's. I—moved in here after he died intending to pack all his things before selling it, but——' she shrugged, 'I stayed instead.' She said nothing about the frantic days and nights when she had coped not only with the loss of her father, but a vastly complicated business empire. She had said too much already. 'I'm afraid I can only ask you in for a quick drink,' she said coolly, leading the way into the elegant living room and crossing to the padded bar set plushly against the far mirrored wall. 'What can I get for you?'

'A little human warmth wouldn't go amiss.'

Fiona swung round, the brows she had pencilled to a darker colour rising frostily. 'I'm sorry, I don't know what you mean.'

What did he expect, this oversized Scotsman who looked as much out of place in this modern setting as a—as a sheepdog at a prize poodle show? If she had thought of him at all during the past two years, it was only as an obstacle to be removed from Glenappon whenever the opportunity presented itself. Perhaps it had come sooner than she had expected.

'I'll take whisky,' he said levelly, 'if you have a decent one.'

Fiona turned back to the bar and reached for a bottle on the upper shelf of the wall behind it. Splashing a generous measure into a squat glass, she crossed back to where he still stood and thrust the glass into his hand.

'It's the most expensive whisky in your country or in mine,' she said sweetly, 'will that do?'

He took his time about tasting it, his eyes never leaving hers, then he nodded. 'It's fine.' There was something maddeningly irritating about the way he sauntered off across the room, appraising as he went the strict symmetry of the furniture, the perfectly displayed art, even peering out at the wide terrace before stepping out on to it.

'Look, Mr—*Roderick*,' Fiona gritted, hurrying after him and finding him leaning on the parapet looking down at the traffic so far below as to be almost noiseless, 'I'm being called for any minute now and I have to leave, so please——'

'Is David the one calling for you?'

She stared at him speechlessly. How in the world had he remembered a name he had heard only in passing over two years ago? 'Yes,' she sighed impatiently, 'and he'll be here any minute now. I'm due to give a speech in——' she lifted her wrist to eye level, 'forty-five minutes from now. Perhaps you'd like to drop by the office tomorrow, I'll be pleased to have someone show you around.'

'That will be a speech for the Travel Agents' Association?' he asked unhurriedly, ignoring her offer of a guided tour of the Mackay building.

Had he been this ponderously slow two years ago in Scotland? Surely she couldn't have spent even ten minutes on a sofa enjoying his lovemaking! That she did remember, but—— Her head jerked round to where he leaned casually, the drink still full in his glass.

'How do you know about that? And how did you know where to find me?'

He smiled lazily, a groove beside his mouth giving her an unexpected pang. 'Your secretary, Mrs Oates, was very helpful on the last point when I told her I had come to see you on Glenappon business. As for your first question, it happens that——'

The doorbell buzzed faintly in the background and he paused.

'Would you like me to answer it?' he asked politely.

'No!' Whirling away, Fiona trod rapidly across the tiled terrace and more slowly through the living room to the hall. What did he mean, 'Glenappon business?'—more to the point, how did it concern her?

In comparison to her unexpected visitor, David's appearance seemed suaver than ever, his black-tie formal outfit emphasising his tanned good looks. He probably paid an exorbitant amount to have his thick light brown hair styled in that deliberately casual look, but it was extremely effective. He stepped into the hall and put his hands lightly on her shoulders as he bent to kiss her cheek.

'You look beautiful, as always,' he complimented, smiling as he straightened up. 'Mmm . . . is that a new perfume you're wearing? A little spicier than your usual, but I like it.'

Embarrassment prompted her quick, 'David, there's someone here with me. It's——' She turned and caught sight of Roderick Cairns standing in the living room entrance, his empty glass clasped in his hand as if he had been there for hours. Darn! He must have seen David's intimate greeting, heard his comment about her perfume that made it clear how familiar he was with her tastes. But what did it matter *what* he thought? He was of the period she had designated mentally as before her father's death . . . her life since then had taken an entirely different turn, made her an entirely different person.

Her eyes cool, she completed the introduction. 'Roderick Cairns of——' she caught herself up before saying 'Glenappon'; she wasn't going to make his standing there official by her own mouth!—'of Scotland. We met while I was there, and he decided to come and look me up in New York while he's here. This is David Warner,' she introduced in more perfunctory manner, 'Chief of Operations for Mackay.'

Roderick's black brows rose in a mocking arc she somehow remembered. Coming forward, he put out a frank hand to shake the other man's, commenting, 'You've had promotion since I last heard of you. Congratulations.' A flicker of amusement lit the eyes he turned from David to her, and Fiona irritatedly read his mind. The queen had raised her prospective consort to appropriate position in the Mackay hierarchy.

'Well, thanks,' David responded in his best consumer relations manner—had she made a mistake in elevating him from the area where he excelled? He never could resist an opportunity to charm, although it wasn't strictly necessary now that his administrative expertise was more important. For once he failed to read the message her eyes conveyed. 'Why don't we have a drink before we leave?' he suggested genially.

'There really isn't time,' she murmured, glancing at her watch significantly.

'Sure there is! It won't take more than ten minutes to get to where we're going, and I'd like to get to know Mr Cairns a little better.' He smiled expansively at Roderick, and Fiona seethed. How easily he succumbed to flattery, being totally blind to the mockery that would have pricked his balloon of self-importance. Maybe that was why——

'All right,' she said abruptly, holding out her hand for Roderick's glass and marching into the living room with it, the two men following. Roderick would have the same again, and David would share her own taste for white wine. The social sounds of the men's conversation bypassed her completely as she refilled her own glass with white wine and took a fresh one for David, then poured a new drink for the man who, despite his outlandish garb, seemed completely at home in the tastefully furnished living room.

'Hey, what do you know?' David enthused as he took his glass from her, 'Roderick here is in New York to attend the thing we're going to tonight! That's really a coincidence.'

'Isn't it?' Fiona thrust his glass into Roderick's hand, her eyes disbelieving as they met the dancing humour in his. What gall to assume that he could just breeze into the affair that had been planned for months! 'I wasn't aware, though, that people unconnected with the travel business had been invited.' Roderick obviously hadn't been, but for reasons of his own he was intent on coming along with them tonight.

'Oh, but I am connected,' he assured them with a politely sarcastic smile. 'It's such a small hotel, I'm not surprised you haven't heard of it. Glenappon Castle Hotel,' he went on levelly, his eyes fixed boldly on Fiona's, 'isn't in the same league as Mackay Hotels, but we've been steadily increasing our business over the past eighteen months. We found that North Americans in particular like the flavour of the old Scotland we provide at Glenappon.'

'Glenappon!' David exclaimed while Fiona was drawing an indignant breath. 'Isn't that your father's old home, the place where you stayed, Fiona, when you went to your uncle's funeral?'

Ignoring him, Fiona stared accusingly at the blandly unconcerned Scot. 'You turned Glenappon into a tourist hotel?' she choked.

'Can you think of a better use for a castle long on history but short on capital funds?' he countered enigmatically, and Fiona recalled her own appraisal of the castle as hotel on her short visit there. But her father would never have agreed to——

'We really should leave,' David interrupted her bitter thoughts, turning to Roderick Cairns with somewhat lessened enthusiasm than he had displayed so far. He was remembering how changed Fiona had been after her visit to Scotland, and a rare flash of intuition had alerted him to the possibility that the confident Scot in their midst might have had something to do with it. Nevertheless, he sensed a boost to Mackay's international revenues in the ambience Glenappon, and other authentic European noble houses, could provide for culture-seeking Americans.

'Why don't you come along with us, Roderick?' he invited cordially. 'It doesn't seem practical for you to go your way and us ours then end up at the same place.'

'Thank you very much.' Roderick pulled his attention from Fiona's appalled expression to the determinedly hospitable David. 'As a matter of fact, I wanted to talk to Fiona about Glenappon, but as you seem to be the head man, perhaps——?' He paused, looking from one to the other of them, and Fiona was unaccountably reminded of his declaration on the day of her uncle's funeral two years before. 'Mother, Fiona has consented to be my wife' or words to that effect. She hadn't spoken up then, but now she had all the confidence of two years of corporate management behind her.

'*I* make the major decisions in this company,' she cut in coldly, disregarding David's pained look. 'We'll talk about Glenappon later.'

The decision, which would have been accepted as gospel by any member of her staff, including David, made little impression on Roderick Cairns.

'That should work out all right,' he agreed with

maddening aplomb, rising and glancing at the watch which would have seemed cumbersome on any other man's wrist. 'I'll be talking to one or two other people tonight about Glenappon, so— oh, I'm sorry, we should be leaving, shouldn't we?'

Fiona glared at him malevolently and shook off the hand he placed solicitously under her arm, gratifying David when she went forward and tucked her hand pointedly in the crook of his arm. The gesture wasn't lost on Roderick, though he seemed more amused than chastened by it.

What nerve! she fumed in silent rage as they left the apartment and walked towards the elevator, Roderick striding ahead in his ridiculous tweeds to press the button and have the doors open when they arrived. Dressed like that, he should have felt some kind of embarrassment in David's impeccable presence; instead, he was mulishly taking over. And his stupid dangling of other prospects for the backing of Glenappon as a hotel was a business trick she had cut her teeth on!

Still, she wondered curiously as she stepped between the two men to enter David's car parked at kerbside, which of Mackay Hotels competitors would be attending the dinner meeting tonight?

CHAPTER FIVE

FIONA was the first speaker after the mandatory chicken dinner, and for once she was ill at ease, too conscious of Roderick Cairns' steady scrutiny. The words her staff had prepared for her to speak seemed trite, and paid only lip service to the problems that plagued the travel industry.

'Now, more than ever,' she concluded thankfully, 'we have to be aware of what the travelling public wants. Our research shows that they want what has always pleased—St. Peter's in Rome, Versailles in France, the Acropolis in Athens.'

'Is there not also,' a voice that was rapidly becoming hatefully familiar spoke up from the white-clothed table facing the dais, 'a swing towards the more offbeat destinations, such as the one I represent at Glenappon in Scotland? It seems to me that many Americans of Scottish extraction would be very happy to spend their tourist dollars visiting the land of their fathers in authentic surroundings.'

A storm of applause greeted his words, revealing a depth of conviction Fiona hadn't been aware of.

'I'm sure Mr Cairns, the representative from Scotland,' she said drily, 'will be pleased to enlighten you later with the charms his Scottish district has to offer, but I'm here to talk about the overall picture of travel in today's world. None of us is unaware of the decline in tourism,' she expanded, purposely avoiding Roderick's eyes. 'Our balance sheets reflect a tight economy, and that means that the travelling public tends to stay closer to home. If they can afford an overseas trip, they want to see the places I've already mentioned. Perhaps in a year or two,' she dismissed lightly Roderick Cairns' bid for a slice of the dwindling market, 'things will be different, but for the moment Americans are heavily into national travel. Last year, for instance, there was an increase of——' she glanced down at the page in front of her, 'twenty-eight per cent in tourists visiting. . . .'

While aware of Roderick's tightlipped expression as she expanded on the flurry of interest in home-grown comforts, she felt a righteous certainty in downgrading the stately-home-turned-tourist attraction he represented. Glenappon belonged by right to her, not to her uncle's stepson. Her father must be turning in his grave at the very idea of strangers waking in the morning, perhaps in his childhood bedroom, looking forward to a huge Scottish breakfast served in the panelled dining room.

The applause for her speech, which she admitted held little immediate hope for burgeoning tourism, rattled like dried leaves around the room. Bradley Stevens, the sixty-year-old head of the unlikely-sounding Pillow Talk hotel chain, spoke after her and received an enthusiastic wave of response when he backed Roderick Cairns' small and simple, authentic historical surroundings, suggestion.

Nibbling on her thumb, she recalled worriedly that Bradley Stevens had sat next to Roderick at dinner and had seemed extraordinarily interested in what the younger man had been saying. But surely not even Roderick Cairns would contemplate Pillow Talk, Glenappon! But who knew?

She looked with narrowed eyes at the Scot and found him staring hard at her. Unspoken messages passed fleetingly between brown eyes and blue . . . suddenly he looked far from bucolic in his thick homespun tweeds. His chin was as grimly determined as she had seen her father's at times, his eyes as bleakly stern as James Mackay's when something was bothering him. Mostly, her father's had looked like that for a long time after her mother's death, but the loss of a loved one couldn't be the reason . . . her eyes went back to his again in question. Had Isabel——? She hadn't enquired about his mother, but it was entirely possible that the death of the older woman could bring that look to his eyes.

'I'd like to leave,' she muttered to David, sitting beside her and seemingly absorbed in what the third speaker was saying.

'We can't leave now!' he expostulated under his breath, giving her an exasperated side glance. 'Carl Landon and Steve Hubrick have to speak yet.'

'Then you stay and listen to them,' she snapped, gathering up her purse and making a quiet departure. They would think she was making a necessary visit to the ladies' room; by the time she was really missed, the speechmaking would be over. David, she knew, would dutifully stay until the last word had been spoken. Good old David, the salt of the business world.

She drew a deep breath of city air on the steps of the auditorium and decided to walk the few blocks to home. She got far too little exercise immured in her office from nine to five each workday, and little more on weekends, apart from a swim in a Long Island host's pool on the odd occasions when she accepted an invitation. David's family, comfortably ensconced at Cape Cod for the summer, had a fetish about keeping fit. If it wasn't a pre-breakfast jog on the beach, it was a marathon competitive swim, neither of which appealed to her. Mostly, she stayed in town on summer weekends, enjoying the treed and shrubbed terrace so high above the traffic that its vague hum was only a minor annoyance.

'Hi, honey.'

Absorbed in her own thoughts, Fiona hadn't sensed the arrival of a battered-looking car that was keeping pace with her unhurried stride. Oh no, why had she forgotten that New York at night was fit for neither man nor beast? The slim lines of her evening purse held nothing more than cosmetics to repair her make-up, but the leering young men leaning from the ancient car weren't to know that.

The car kept pace with her lengthened stride, then suddenly it drew ahead and jerked to a stop. Shadowy figures, she couldn't see how many, erupted from the vehicle and slouched around her. Nervously, she walked on.

'Hey, honey,' a laughing voice said beside her, 'what's the hurry? The night is young and you're very beautiful.'

The words were corny, but the intent was only too clear. The contents of her purse didn't interest them; she herself did. Fiona lengthened her stride, her eyes scanning the deserted street for a taxi. This couldn't be happening to her ... but it was. A strangled squeal rose in her throat as a hard young hand was laid on her arm, jerking her round to face a tangle-haired youth who grinned down at her arrogantly, hitching his spare thumb into the belt of his well-worn jeans.

'What's the matter?' he demanded. 'Think you're too good for me or something?'

'Yes, I am,' she retorted with the boldness of fear. 'Take your hand off me. . . .'

His hand was indeed lifted suddenly from her arm, but she made no pause to congratulate herself. Her eyes watched strickenly as a tweed-clad arm came between herself and her assailant, and she almost found it in herself to pity him as his head cracked back and he uttered an oath she had only read in kitchen sink novels. Almost, but not quite.

'Thank you,' she said shakily to Roderick Cairns, who had dispatched not only her would-be lover but his cohorts, who dived back into the ancient car and clung to its steel doorposts as it roared off into the night.

'What in heaven's name possessed you to walk alone on the streets of New York?' he demanded irascibly, his hand implacably firm on her elbow as he thrust her towards the more brightly lighted avenue where traffic plied as busily as it did in broad daylight.

'I—I didn't want to stay and listen to any more speeches,' Fiona explained weakly, shaken by the encounter more than she would have cared to admit. 'I didn't know——'

'As a woman living in New York,' he cut in savagely, his arm raised and miraculously summoning a taxi, 'you should have known that it's not safe to walk the streets alone. What in hell,' he demanded as he handed her into the taxi, 'did you think those young punks wanted? To exchange addresses with you?'

Breath eased in nervously controlled gasps from Fiona's throat as she slid into the cab and across to the far side, leaving room for Roderick to climb in beside her.

Briskly, he gave her address to the uninterested driver and leaned back, his face still angrily pale in the flashing reflection of street lights.

'I—I really didn't think,' she ventured by way of apology. 'It's not far. . . .' she shrugged. His mouth was as tightly clamped as ever when she darted another glance at him. Stiffly, she went on, 'Anyway, thanks a lot for your help.'

He gave her a searing look. 'What in hell was Warner thinking of to let you walk off into the night like that, alone?'

'It wasn't David's fault,' she defended. 'He said I should stay for the rest of the speeches, but I. . . .' She had needed to get out into the fresh air and think, but she couldn't expect someone like Roderick Cairns to understand that, particularly since he himself was the prime cause of her unsettled mood. To drop that bombshell about Glenappon just as they were leaving the apartment, and then to talk cosily with Bradley Stevens as if emphasising that there was competition as backer of the Glenappon Castle Hotel! Glenappon was hers by right of inheritance, and she'd be damned if she'd see, even in her imagination, a sign that read: *Pillow Talk, Glenappon Castle!* Besides that . . . the hard tensing of his thigh muscle against her much softer one was reminding her of sensations she thought she had dismissed permanently from her mind.

The driver evidently agreed with her that the distance was short; Roderick cut short his complaints with a bill thrust into his hand, whereupon he became as close to ingratiating as a New York cabby could come.

There was no question of Roderick coming into the apartment with her. As if it were his right to do so, he took the keys from her hand and ushered her inside. Accepting that he intended to stay for a while when he closed the door firmly behind them, she went ahead into the living room and crossed to the bar after throwing her purse on the neatly aligned chair just inside the entrance.

'I think we need a drink,' she took up her stance behind the padded leather bar and looked at him enquiringly. 'What will you have? I think I'll have whisky.'

'That's fine,' he nodded, looking at her curiously as he came to perch on one of the matching leather bar-stools. 'It must cost quite a bit to keep this as well stocked as you do.'

Hah! He was probing in a roundabout way to find out how much she herself drank. The truth was, apart from a little white wine, the bar didn't normally interest her. In fact, she hadn't tasted whisky since the day of her uncle's funeral, when Roderick himself had pressed it on her. Most of the bottles lining the shelves had been laid in by her father, but some imp of mischief advised her to keep that fact to herself.

'Fortunately, I don't have to worry about the liquor bill,' she said lightly, taking down two pristine clear whisky glasses and adding a generous measure to each. 'It's written off to entertainment.'

'I see.' Roderick lifted his glass to toast, 'Here's to the success of Glenappon Castle Hotel.'

'Don't you mean Pillow Talk, Glenappon Castle?' she enquired tartly, coming round to perch on the stool next to his.

'Not necessarily.' A glint lit the dark depths of his eyes as he sipped on the rich brown liquid. 'That depends on you.'

'Does it?' she asked levelly, disliking the spiritous fumes of the whisky but drinking it anyway. 'You know I wouldn't willingly let Glenappon descend to the level of the Pillow Talk hotel chain,' she said bitterly, 'so what's your price?'

'Price?' The long, thin fingers she suddenly remembered against a car wheel caressed the straight sides of the whisky glass. 'I've no wish to put a price on Glenappon, but it's a fact of life that the estate cannot support itself. Fergus, your uncle, disagreed with my suggestion of a hotel, yet he knew when he left Glenappon to me that that was exactly what I would do with it.' He looked bleakly into her eyes. 'The income from lumber, properly harvested, brings in too little to make the estate a viable proposition. Some other means of self-support was necessary if Glenappon wasn't to become a mouldering relic of better Highland days, and I've chosen this alternative.

'We have done comparatively well in the short time we've been operating, but we need the backing of a corporation such as Mackay Hotels or,' he paused and looked down at his glass, 'the Pillow Talk Corporation.'

An idea took root in Fiona's mind. Why hadn't she thought of it before? 'There's absolutely no need for Glenappon to be turned into a hotel at all,' she said crisply. 'As I'm a Mackay, it rightly belongs to me, but I'd be willing to buy it from you if the price is right.'

She frowned when he shook his head without a vestige of regret.

'No, Glenappon was left in my care.' His eyes blazed suddenly into hers, searing her with their intensity. 'For pity's sake, Fiona, whould you have it become a holiday residence whenever you could snatch a week or two away from Mackay Hotels business? Glenappon was meant to be lived in, to nurture the children who will one day nurture it!'

Abstractedly, Fiona wished she could harness that kind of passion and mete it out to her marketing managers. Mackay Hotels would leap to prominence on the stock market! On a more realistic level, she realised that Roderick would never relinquish Glenappon, for however much money. She had to tread warily, make him believe that Mackay Hotels was the only corporation to lend money and prestige to his fledgling hotel. What could be better than a Mackay to run the hotel that had been in the Mackay family for generations? It would only be a matter of time until Fiona Mackay took complete control. Then it wouldn't be a Mackay Hotels enterprise, it would be the proud country home of Fiona Mackay and her consort.

David? Somehow she couldn't see him as Laird of Glenappon, but perhaps he would settle down when he knew that, if he was her husband, respect and adulation would come his way as a matter of course. There would still be the vast empire of Mackay Hotels to run, and who better than David to do that?

'So what do you think?' Roderick broke tersely into her daydreaming thoughts. 'I would, of course, insist that you came back to Glenappon and see the potential for yourself.'

It was the first step towards the realisation of her dream, and Fiona hesitated only momentarily before saying, 'All right. We'll come over there and——'

'*We?*' he interrupted brusquely, his eyes hard as they bored across into hers.

Fiona looked at him with eyes rounded in surprise. 'Of course. I wouldn't dream of making such a decision without David's expert opinion. I'll let you know when we're both free to come over and take a look at Glenappon with a view to making it a Mackay Hotel.'

Roderick stood up and laid his half-empty glass on the padded bar. 'Good,' he said crisply, 'I just hope you'll find yourselves free before Bradley

Stevens does—he's made a definite commitment for August the fifteenth.'

'I'm not intimidated by threats to go elsewhere for backing for Glenappon,' she lied, rising too and confronting him with cheeks reddened by irritation. He was acting like some wayward tycoon instead of the cap-in-hand suppliant he was.

'Aren't you?'

She regarded him mutinously, feeling at a disadvantage as her medium height forced her to look up into the storming brown of his eyes. 'No, I'm not. David knows all there is to know about client potential. . . .'

'Does he?'

The terse question was accompanied by a wide sweep of a tweed-clad arm that pulled her hard against the taut fitness of his implacable body. 'Does he also know all there is to know about the woman he wants to marry?' Roderick demanded fiercely, the burn of his eyes glowing on the neat conformation of her hair in its neat chignon arrangement. 'For instance,' his fingers swept ruthlessly up and loosed one hairpin after another so that her hair fell in a jerky golden tumble about her shoulders, 'does he know that you're the most beautiful woman in the world when your hair's down like this—it's like spun gold,' he wondered, letting it drift through his fingers, his jaw hardening again as he sought the bewildered blue of her eyes. 'Does he ever make love to you like this?'

Her response was lost in the more immediate swiftness of his kiss, the demanding quest of lips that grew soft then hard on the surprised softness of her own. She wanted to resist, to repel the insistent sensations that clamoured at her senses, but something that was weak in her responded to the firm insistence of his mouth. Her own moulded to its firm outlines, and her hands seemed exquisitely sensitive suddenly to the rough wool of his jacket, the smooth white of his shirt as it rose to encircle the broad column of his neck. The high line of her instep arched further as her toes curled under into her delicately fashioned shoes, and she forgot without regret about David's chaste kisses.

Every nerve end in her body seemed to be pulsing with an awareness she had never recognised before. It seemed entirely right that her fingers should curl into the soft thickness of hair at his neck, as if every silken strand was familiar to her. In the same way, the fit of breast and hip and thigh to the overpowering maleness of Roderick's hard physique seemed pre-ordained. . . .

The outer doorbell had been ringing for longer than she cared to consider when she drew away at last, her eyes clinging to the bruised brown of his.

'Roderick, I——' She should make some declaration of love, or some explanation for her abandoned response to his lovemaking. But how could she when his lips were tracing evocative paths along the sensitive cords connecting her head to the rest of her body?

As it happened, it was Roderick who pushed her from him and said huskily, 'Go and let your lapdog in and tell him you're coming alone to Glenappon.'

Fiona seemed to be floating in a soft warm sea as she crossed to the hall and the insistently ringing bell. Only when she reached the hall did she realise that she had obeyed him without thinking, as a junior member of her staff would have carried out any command of her own. Even her fingers seemed nervelessly incapable as they made a useless attempt to smooth the wild tumble of her hair. What would David, if it were he at the door, think of that and the obvious fact that she had just been kissed almost to insensibility? Drawing a deep, calming breath, she opened the door.

'I was beginning to think something had happened to you on the way home.' David marched in confidently, pausing as his shocked eyes took in her dishevelled appearance. 'My God!' he ejaculated softly, 'what happened to you? I've—never seen you with your hair down like that and looking so . . . so beautiful. Were you getting ready for bed?'

'No, I—David, there's someone——'

There was no time to finish the sentence. David unexpectedly drew her to him and kissed her mouth with more ardour than he had ever shown before . . . the mouth that was still warm from Roderick's kisses. Desperately, Fiona tried to pull herself away from his ardent arms, wishing she could give vent to the hysterical laughter bubbling in her throat. It was too funny. Generally, her life continued on an evenly composed tenor, and here, in one evening, she had two men in her apartment intent on ravaging her!

'For heaven's sake, David, let me go!'

'It might be better if *I* go, Fiona.'

With Roderick's softly spoken words, Fiona's struggle ended. David's arms dropped to his sides and his mouth fell open unbecomingly as he stared at the other man, commanding the entrance to the living room.

'You!'

'Yes!' Fiona flared, wishing both of them would disappear from her sight and leave her to sort out her chaotic thoughts. 'If it hadn't been for him, I could have been found in an alley somewhere tomorrow morning!—while you listened to long, boring speeches.'

Without enquiring about what had happened, David turned defensive eyes on her. 'How did I know you were going to run off like that? As it happened, it was very important that one of us stay and hear what went on. Did you know that Bradley Stevens of Pillow Talk is expanding his operation in Europe? He's bought a castle on the Rhine, a château in France, and now he's thinking of——'

'That's exactly what Mr—Roderick and I were discussing when you arrived,' she interrupted coolly, feeling suddenly weary as she walked past Roderick into the living room. Both men followed her. 'Bradley's obviously collecting a chain of stately homes with a view to reaching the only market with money at this time,' she thought aloud, kicking off her shoes before curving her slender legs under her on one of the clear-cut sofas.

'Mind if I pour myself a drink?' David asked, scarcely waiting for her hand wave towards the bar before going to it and pouring a generous measure from the whisky bottle still on its leather top. Roderick remained standing to one side of it, the drink Fiona had poured still gleaming amber through his fingers.

'Why don't we do the same thing?' David suggested, taking a long gulp at his glass and loosening his tie slightly as he dropped to the other end of the sofa. 'There must be dozens of big houses available at a reasonable price. Some of these old families are long on history but very short on cash right now.' As if remembering that Roderick had no connection with the inner workings of the Mackay chain, he added awkwardly. 'But maybe we should discuss it in your office tomorrow.'

Certainly it would have been better to mull company business over in private, Fiona thought abstractedly, but Roderick was fully aware of her wish to keep Glenappon a Mackay affair. It might push his eventual price up considerably, knowing her obsession, but that was a normal hazard of business.

'There's no need for that,' she said crisply, her mind working in its usual precise pattern at last. 'Bradley Stevens is actively interested in Glenappon Castle as one of his stately homes, but I'd like to take a look at it myself before anything is finalised.' That was sufficiently noncommittal, she thought, to tone down her bid for Glenappon. Roderick's eyes, so deep and dark in his lean face, met hers blandly.

'I'm sure you'll see the potential of Glenappon once you're there,' he said gravely.

Anger rose and threatened to choke Fiona. The potential of Glenappon! How dared he? Glenappon was hers by blood-right, and there could be no greater claim. But ... she calmed herself deliberately ... no purpose would be served by venting her righteous anger. Every man, including Roderick Cairns, had his price. Money wasn't important; Glenappon was.

Doubtfully, David interposed, 'Well, I guess I could postpone my vacation for a while.' He was spending the month of August, Fiona recalled, at his parents' mountain home in Colorado.

'There's no need for that,' she squashed firmly. 'If I decide that Glenappon is right for us, I'll get in touch with you. Now, if you don't mind,' she unfolded her legs and stood up wearily, 'I'd like to get some rest now. Where are you staying, Mr — Roderick?' she turned coolly towards him, as if her blood hadn't sung in her veins such a short time ago when he had held her in his arms.

The hotel he named wasn't familiar to her.

'I'll be in touch about the arrangements to visit Glenappon,' she followed both men into the hall, relieved that they had received the message that neither was welcome to stay longer.

Roderick, she mused as she readied herself for bed, had spoken hardly at all after David's arrival. But strangely, his presence had been forceful enough without words.

She paused before sliding her filmy peach nightdress over her head. He affected her as no other man ever had . . . here and at Glenappon. He was rough compared with David's sophisticated charm, but David had never made every nerve in her body respond to his male charisma.

When all was said and done, she reflected as she slid under the covers of the bed she used only in part, he was still a man with an axe to grind. The Glenappon he obviously loved would flourish and survive for another generation, given the benefits of Mackay wealth. . . .

Apart from a hazy sun enveloping the distant spires and solid buildings of Edinburgh, everything was as she previously remembered from her visit to the land of her fathers. The Customs and Immigration officials were different yet reminiscent of the ones who had first greeted her on her arrival two years before.

A weakness attacked Fiona's knees when she at last emerged into the arrival hall, knowing that this time there would be a familiar face to greet her. And there he was, waiting stoically beyond the barrier, his eyes scanning each released passenger until they met hers. Knowing how ridiculous her pleasure was at seeing him again—yes, dressed in the kilt that left his well-shaped knees and calves open for inspection—Fiona dragged her attention from him and gave a brilliant smile to the distinguished-looking man who had shared the transatlantic journey with her.

'Can you see your wife?' she asked, still smiling.

'I can,' he returned solemnly, hiding in his peculiarly Scottish way his delight at meeting the wife and sons he had been parted from for almost a year.

'And you?'

'Yes.' Her eyes swivelled back to Roderick's broodingly solemn face. 'Yes, my party's here.'

The American expression seemed an odd one as she walked, encumbered with her heavy suitcase, towards Roderick. A black frown sliced down between his dark brows, and his mouth was a compressed line as he took her luggage from her.

'I'm sorry the plane was a little late,' she apologised, feeling vaguely let down by his brusque welcome, which consisted of a distant nod and a hard grasp of fingers at her elbow as he guided her out of the airport.

'I was a bit late myself, so I hadn't been waiting long.'

That was the sum total of their conversation

until they were settled in the familiar station wagon and on their way out of the airport environs.

Even without the too-heavy foot on the brake pedal as they approached a stop light, Fiona was uncomfortably aware of his dour mood. It made her own lightness of spirit crossing the Atlantic seem stupidly juvenile. She had actually looked forward with tingling awareness to seeing him again, and had honestly admitted that Glenappon had little or nothing to do with it. She glanced sideways at him when he set the vehicle in motion again, her eyes flashing irritation.

'Look,' she began, 'I'm here to——'

'Who was he?' he interrupted coldly, his eyes intent on the road ahead.

Fiona stared. 'What?'

'The man you travelled with,' he elaborated grimly.

'The man——? Oh, you mean. . . .' Her irritation dissolved into thoughtfulness. Could he possibly be jealous of the stranger on the plane? If so, he had no right to be that possessive. 'Oh, he's just one of the men I have quickie affairs with on planes. You should try it, the time passes so much quicker. Unfortunately, he was being met by his wife and grown sons, and I was being met by you, so there was no opportunity to extend our passionate encounter.'

Her question as to his sense of humour or lack of it was answered when she glanced at him again and saw a reluctant smile tugging at his very well-shaped mouth. His eyes, too, held a faint glimmer of sheepish amusement.

'From the way you smiled at him, it seemed to me he was someone you knew very well.'

'Aren't you being a little too interested in my personal life?'

'Aren't you forgetting,' he paused while he overtook some slow moving traffic, 'that as you are my future wife your personal life interests me very much?'

Fiona sat up abruptly. 'Your *what*?'

'Had you forgotten that we became engaged to marry on the day of your uncle's funeral?' he countered with maddening calm, seemingly unaware of Fiona's unattractively dropped jaw.

He must be mad, she decided; in which case, she was in a dangerous position. Driving in a car with a maniac hadn't come into her orbit of experience so far, and she wasn't about to jump out on the disorientating left side of the road, which was the way they drove in Britain. Besides, they were crossing an impressively long bridge which she surmised abstractedly must be the famous Forth Bridge, one she seemed to have missed entirely on her first drive up to Glenappon in the Highlands. Wouldn't it be best to humour him until they reached their destination?

'Yes ... yes, of course I remember it,' she only partially lied. Isabel had discovered them making love on the couch in her uncle's office on the day of his funeral. The older woman's shocked face was still vivid in her memory ... but had she agreed to marry the strong-thighed Scot by her side? Everything about the rest of that day was hazy in her memory ... all she recalled was Roderick snatching the black telephone from her, her own eruption of tears against his shirt front.

'Good,' Was the sidelong look he gave her disbelieving? Perhaps just a little sceptical? 'My mother is taking great pleasure in arranging everything, but you must feel free to express your own wishes.'

'Yes,' Fiona said faintly, wishing futilely that she had brought David along. With him in the rear seat, this ridiculous conversation wouldn't be taking place. Marry Roderick! She hardly knew him, so why would she think of pledging her life to him? True, he knew how to rouse her in a physical sense, and in a way David had never even attempted to, but between the two men she would choose David every time. He was comfortable in her world, and she was comfortable with him. Why in the world would she think of plunging herself into a life that was alien to her every experience? Glenappon was as far removed from the Mackay Hotels milieu in New York as it was possible to be. David understood the complexities of hotel chain management, Roderick was a firmly cemented Scotsman whose life was bounded by Glenappon.

Not even the realisation that she was weighing the two men in the balance, as if such a thing were necessary, could prevent the droop of her eyelids towards her creamy smooth cheeks. Flying always affected her adversely, leaving her uninterested in the problems that plagued her . . . even the one of sharing a station wagon with a madman.

CHAPTER SIX

FIONA paced the room restlessly, the scent of summer flowers, scattered in profusion in urns and vases, filling her nostrils and giving her a heady feeling that made it difficult to think clearly.

The room was the same one she had occupied two years before, yet she was far more distraught now than she had been then, despite the solemnity of that occasion. Isabel had greeted her in much the same way, but it was what she said afterwards, in the lofty coolness of the stone-flagged hall, that echoed and re-echoed in Fiona's mind.

'I can't tell you how happy I am that you've come back,' the older woman enthused, her dark eyes, so like her son's, expressive of her contentment. 'You'll find some changes in Glenappon, but I've no doubt you'll have your own ideas about things after you and Roderick are married.'

Changes were only too apparent, from Catriona's sulky welcome from behind a newly installed reception desk to the thick replacement of threadbare carpet by warmly gleaming red broadloom on the broad sweep of stairs leading to the upper level.

'Catriona acts as receptionist,' Isabel explained as she accompanied Fiona up the foot-sinking stairs of expensive carpeting. 'Our American visitors seem to love the welcome she gives them.'

Not if her welcome was as cold as the one she's just given me, Fiona thought grimly as she mounted the stairs behind Isabel's much trimmer hips in pleated beige and pink skirt. The added exercise of helping run a hotel had definitely slimmed the older woman's figure.

The portraits lining the upper hall had received a facelift too. Gilt now gleamed dully in frames encompassing early Mackays. There was a general air of genteel prosperity to dispel the previous lingering atmosphere of musty stagnation. Even without the embellishments Mackay Hotels could provide, Fiona recognised that Glenappon now offered something no ordinary high-rise concrete could. Ambience ... the catchword of present marketing techniques. History lurked in every broad corridor, every unexpected flight of stairs leading to who knew where.

Mad he might be in a matrimonial sense, but Roderick Cairns knew instinctively what would appeal to Americans hungering for a taste of elegant ancestral living.

'You won't mind if we move you to the east side of the house in two weeks, will you?' Isabel asked worriedly as they entered the familiar room, more fulsome now because of the flowers. 'Mr van Pelt of—where was it now?—Long Island, I think, or was it New Jersey? Anyway, he wants to take this room and the one adjoining for himself and his two children. Being in the hotel business yourself, Fiona, I'm sure you will understand. . . .'

'Being in a smaller room won't bother me at all,' Fiona retorted irritably. 'What does bother me is——'

'Of course, when you and Roderick marry, you will be moving into the main suite that looks out over the lake,' Isabel prattled on, her hands busily rearranging the wide bowl of shaggy headed flowers on the dresser more to her satisfaction, 'or as we call it here, the loch. Roderick, of course, would never consider using that as part of the hotel. It's hardly recognisable now, so much work has been done to it, and most of it by Roderick himself.' She turned and smiled mistily at Fiona, going on softly, 'You might say it was a labour of love, knowing he would be sharing it with you.'

It was like floating on a sea of insubstantial cotton that enveloped her smotheringly every time she tried to voice a protest, to stop this ridiculous farce before it went any further, but at last Isabel paused for breath.

'Look, Isabel,' she got in quickly, 'Roderick knew no such——'

'Did I hear my name?' he asked from the open door, and Fiona gave a smothered exclamation of fury. It was as if he and his mother were engaged in a conspiracy to prevent her saying what was on her mind. Perhaps they were both mad—did the genes of insanity run in families? Hysteria tinged the vision that sprang into her mind of herself borne on the tide of their implacable certainty to a wedding aisle and that marriage suite Roderick had eerily been working on . . . all without having voiced a word of protest.

But this was the twentieth century, not the barbaric ages when women were given in marriage as pawns in a more important game. And, she noted, Roderick looked far from mad as he strolled across the room and dropped a proprietorial kiss on her cheek, his hands sliding down her forearms to clasp with dry warmth round her own.

'Will you please tell your mother,' she said frigidly, her eyes sparking their stormy message into his, 'that——'

'Och,' he smiled, and slid an arm up around her waist, moulding her side to his, 'Fiona's having a case of bridal nerves, Mother. I think it might be better if we don't prolong the agony by waiting too long to make it official.'

Fiona, to her later chagrin, heeded the warning in the sudden sharp pressure of his fingers into her side.

'I'm sure the Minister,' Isabel responded happily,

'will be pleased to perform the ceremony at any time, although,' she frowned worriedly, 'we have to give the guests enough notice to let them make their arrangements. It couldn't be done in under two weeks, Roderick.'

Fiona's disbelieving gasp was ignored as the two planned her immediate future. It was like a nightmare she must wake from soon.

'Then let's set the date for—oh, the thirtieth of August,' Roderick suggested, his hand still firm on her waist as he looked down at Fiona. 'How will that suit you, Fiona?' Without giving her a chance to do more than gasp for air, he looked at his mother and suggested, 'Leave us now, Mother, while we talk about it.'

'Yes, of course,' Isabel agreed with belated tact, retreating to the door, then looking back. 'You'll be down for tea, won't you?'

'We will.'

The older woman had no sooner gone, closing the door behind her, than Fiona jumped, hopping mad, away from Roderick's blandly assertive figure.

'How dare you,' she spluttered, 'how dare you presume that—that I'd go along with your crazy notions? What does it take to get the message through to you—and your mother? I do not now, nor have I ever, entertained the possibility of marriage with you!' She waved a hand that seemed more eloquent than the words she could summon up. 'This whole thing is ridiculous—it's like a bad novel, too unbelievable to be true!'

Roderick's expression, she noted as she swung back from her restless stamp to the window overlooking the rose garden in full bloom, was no longer bland. His eyes were as bleak as she imagined the lake—*loch*—would be in winter, his jaw carved from the granite of the hills surrounding that loch. Yet his voice still held the soft quality of his Highland heritage when he spoke.

'For a businesswoman, you are remarkably romantic,' he commented evenly. 'Unfortunately, this is not a light novel to be read in a spare hour or two. Glenappon is far more important than that. Long before you or I were thought of, this estate was administered by men who cared about it, cared about *you*, though they would never know of your existence. Wars were fought around it, battles lost and won, all because Mackay men were determined to hold on to what belonged to them, to hand down a proud heritage to their descendants.'

He disdained the many surfaces there were to sit upon, preferring to stroll across to the windows at the far side of the room, looking moodily out of them while Fiona, weaker, folded her trembling legs on to the blue and gold coverlet of the bed. His words provoked evocative memories of her father, conjuring up many bedside nights when he had spoken, as fiercely as Roderick did now, of the heritage that was his . . . hers.

'Glenappon Castle has survived jealous raids from local sects and clans,' he went on, 'and fought off every manner of misfortune, but now. . . .' his profile was sharply etched against the diamond-paned window, 'now there's another kind of war. A war against decay and disuse, a war against the poverty that threatens to make Glenappon a ruined monument to times past.' His wild stare was filled with a passionate fervour when he swung round and looked at her. 'I won't allow that to happen, Fiona. You must marry me and make Glenappon safe for our children and theirs.'

'Aren't you forgetting that our children's name would be Cairns, not Mackay?' she questioned, as if cold-bloodedly discussing marriage were an everyday occurrence for her. On a deeper, more emotional level, a vagrant warmth responded not only to his plea for Glenappon, but to the man himself. She wasn't in love with him ... whatever that meant. She wasn't even sure there was such a thing as the heart-pounding emotion she had read and heard of. Certainly it had never bothered her when David, the only man she had seriously considered marrying, departed on his business trips of varying length ... she was always mildly happy when he returned, but—was that love?

'What they're called isn't important,' Roderick dismissed impatiently, bringing her mind back to the subject at hand. 'They can take the name of Mackay-Cairns, it's done all the time. What is important,' he came stiffly across and sat awkwardly beside her on the bed, its wide canopy enclosing them like the roof of a chapel, 'is that you agree to marry me. You're the only one who can save Glenappon.'

Humour came shakily to Fiona's rescue. 'This isn't the most romantic proposal I've ever had!'

'Our marriage would be as romantic as we care to make it,' he said with a briskness that appalled even her businesslike nature. Then his voice dropped a level and became more human. 'We could learn to love each other, Fiona.'

Was love something a person learned? Obviously he thought it was a possibility. Her eyes seemed unnaturally wide when his fingers took her chin and turned her face to his, so that every pore of his dark-jawed face was visible to her. She could imagine the impatience with which he shaved the black-sprouting beard that gave his chin a dark cast an hour after he had run the razor across it. The strong, proud hook of his nose was forgotten in the search for his deepset eyes, with their shading between brown and black. His mouth, well-shaped without being effeminate, was the part of him she remembered most clearly. That, and his lean-fingered capable hands.

'We're not exactly indifferent to each other now, are we?' he asked huskily, one finger going deliberately to describe an outline on the sensitive contours of her lips, bringing a swift indraw of breath from her that made him smile slightly in a satisfied way.

Repelled, Fiona stood up quickly, his hand falling away. 'People don't get married on the strength of a kiss or two,' she said crisply, turning when he rose to go and stand at the window overlooking the colour-laden rose garden. It was easier to say furiously from there, 'I resent being manipulated in this way. Why couldn't you have made this proposal in New York, instead of wasting my time on an unnecessary journey?' She swung round to face him, the flush of anger brightening her cheeks. 'There was never any question of Bradley Stevens and Pillow Talk coming to Glenappon, was there?'

'No,' he admitted simply. 'But would you have come without that spur of competition?'

Fiona glared at him in speechless contempt before sputtering, 'Darn right I wouldn't have come! I've met some sharp operators in my business life, but you, Roderick Cairns, take pride of place! You think because I reacted to your lovemaking—oh yes, I admit I did that!—that all you had to do to get your hands on Mackay money was to lift a little finger and I'd fall into your arms. Your mother's in it too, isn't she?' she put bitterly, swinging back to gaze unseeingly at the neatly kept rosebeds. 'She could stay here in the style she's accustomed——' Her voice broke off sharply when Roderick, crossing the carpeted floor silently, spun her round to face the marblelike hardness in his eyes. Air seemed trapped below her throat, although it was the flesh of her shoulders his fingers dug into, not her neck.

'My mother knows nothing about this,' he said savagely, 'except that I want to marry you. And her only motive in wanting me to marry is so that she'll have grandchildren to dandle on her knee before she's too old to appreciate them. As for Mackay money,' he threw her contemptuously from him but still held her with the fury in his eyes, 'we can manage very well without it. Fergus was against my idea of a hotel, but I can make it work, given time. I thought you cared about Glenappon, about your Scottish heritage, but it seems I was mistaken.' He strode with awesome majesty to the door before turning back to say tightly, 'I'll make arrangements for your return journey to America as soon as possible.'

Fiona stared at the door he slammed behind him for long moments, her emotions more mixed up than she had ever known them. Who did he think he was to speak to her in that overbearing way? All her life, people had deferred to Fiona ... house servants, school friends whose fathers inhabited a lesser stratum in the business world, Mackay Hotels staff who leapt to obey her slightest command.

Darn him!... the roses were still in the full

flush of beauty when she turned back to them, their yellow-gold, pink, crimson, salmon petals rebuking her with their obedient perfection. They knew their role in life, and didn't question the rightness of their environment. Perhaps they longed for a warmer sun than Glenappon could provide, but this was where fate had ordained they spend their lives. And what glorious lives they were, beautiful and heedless of the sharp vagaries of Highland weather.

But it wasn't like that with people, she thought wistfully, watching the fitful play of light from half-cloudy skies as it touched and moved over the brilliant mosaic of colour. The roses were luckier than she; they knew their place and made the best of the circumstances they found themselves in. Where was her place in life? Head of a vast conglomerate, impersonal because of its tentacle-like spread across the civilised nations of the world? Or here at Glenappon, where time moved slowly and in rhythm with nature?

'Oh dear,' she said aloud, and wandered back to the bed whose coverlet still bore the distinct imprints of her own and Roderick's occupation. If only he had hinted—only hinted—that he was in love with her, it would have cast a whole new complexion on his proposal of marriage. Just a little human softness, a promise of future happiness, would have made the difference.

Yet wouldn't her father have wanted her to keep Glenappon as a Mackay heritage? Business man that he was, would he have cared that his daughter would enter a loveless marriage with a man she scarcely knew? No, James Mackay was as devoid of sentiment in business matters as Roderick himself was. To them, one plus one equalled a

satisfactory mathematical equation ... one
Mackay wife plus one Cairns owner of Glenappon
equalled a continuation of the Mackay strain.
And, imbued with her father's nostalgic reminisc-
ences of his Scottish heritage, Fiona knew that she
would marry Roderick.

She knew herself well, knew that her dead
father's wishes were still hers ... for his sake, she
would marry Roderick. Neither man would have
understood the warm salty tears that filled her
eyes, the part of her that craved the moonlight and
roses, the stampeding pulse at the touch of her
beloved. She would marry Roderick, joined only in
their mutual need to preserve Glenappon's
heritage.

Mindful of his promise to arrange her speedy
departure from the land of her forebears, Fiona
rushed to the door and wrenched it open.

The wedding dress, imported from Edinburgh,
had a stiff backing of white taffeta under a
heavy overlay of delicately pointed lace. Pale
yellow rosebuds comprised Fiona's wedding bouquet, the colour echoed in the deeper yellow of
the flowers carried by her attendants ... a
sulkily reluctant Catriona, the niece of Lady
Carstairs captured for the occasion, and the tall
dark and willowy daughter of an adjoining
historic family.

Fiona herself was unaware of the dramatic
picture she made as she advanced with measured
tread down the short aisle of the Glenappon
Church. Her hair flamed against the pristine white
of the headdress Isabel had produced, and her eyes
seemed a cooler, starker blue as they met
Roderick's, turned to her from the end of the aisle

where he stood tall beside Craig Jameson, his best man.

The solemn tones of the Reverend John Russell faded into the background as Fiona made her vows to the man who stood staunchly at her side. Under the dark suit that faithfully followed the broad outline of his shoulders, the smooth indentation of his waist and hips, what was he feeling? Did he regret the loving women who might have stood by his side? Catriona? If her love for Roderick equalled the hatred she had shown towards Fiona, then she did love him greatly.

Fiona had been too numb to sensation for the past two weeks to let the venomous barbs of the dark girl penetrate too deeply. Isabel's happy excitement similarly flowed over her, so obviously so that the older woman tackled her hesitantly one morning at breakfast.

'I hope you won't think I'm interfering, Fiona, but——' she paused, her brown eyes fluttering back to Fiona's distantly set expression, 'well, I can't help noticing . . . are you sure you're quite happy about being married so quickly? Perhaps some of your friends could have come from America if there had been more notice. . . .'

Fiona had stared at her like one coming out of a dream. 'I'm sure,' she said flatly, making some excuse to leave the table, but Isabel's words lingered with her as she walked down to the loch and wandered idly along its edge. Friends! It was a shock to realise how out of touch she had become with her friends in the past few years. There had always been the pressure of business as an excuse—which of them would have considered coming thousands of miles, anyway, to see her married? It was a sobering thought that her future was to be bound up by ties to a man who would become intimate but not personal. . . .

Intimacy . . . how easy it had been to avoid intimate moments with Roderick in the past two weeks, despite his mother's tactful leaving after an hour in the small sitting room each evening. Her own excuses of tiredness, a shopping trip the next day, had been accepted calmly enough by Roderick, who seemed content to play the waiting game. . . .

'I now pronounce you man and wife,' the Minister intoned in a happier voice than he had used before. 'You may kiss your bride, Roderick,' he added informally, beaming as Roderick turned and pulled the stiff Fiona against him, his dark eyes glowing with an inner light as he bent his mouth to hers. His lips were warm, eager like a boy's, and Fiona knew that the waiting game was over. Tonight there would be no calm acceptance of avoiding tactics. A shiver ran icy fingers down her spine, but there was no time to dwell on the after as they were ushered into the vestry to sign the register, a tear-filled Isabel pressing a damp cheek to Fiona's and whispering,

'He's a good man, and I know you'll make each other happy.'

Back down the aisle, her hand poised lightly in the crook of Roderick's arm, faces smiling on either side, the hired photographer wildly snapping pictures as they stood at the church entrance, the last-minute run into the stately Rolls that served for weddings as well as funerals, a smile still pasted on Fiona's face when Roderick turned her to him and kissed her long and deeply. A roar of approval came from behind as the stately car went into motion on the short journey to Glenappon, intensifying when Fiona put her hand round Roderick's neck as if to prolong the kiss. It seemed expected, but as soon as the car turned sharp left to ascend to the castle, Fiona removed her hand and sat back against the upholstery that smelled of stale perfume and tobacco smoke.

'What time are we leaving for Edinburgh?' she asked smoothly, looking outside the car to where yellow and mauve wildflowers bloomed defiantly in the sparse earth between the rocks. 'I should call David, and——'

'You won't be calling David,' Roderick broke in with unexpected harshness, 'not today or ever. As your husband, I'll be overseeing the business affairs of Mackay Hotels. You'll be busy making a home for us here at Glenappon, and helping to run the hotel until our family comes along. Then, of course, you'll have plenty to occupy yourself with.'

Fiona drew one deep breath, then another. 'Darn you!' she breathed as the car drew into the forecourt of Glenappon. 'Just because I've married you it doesn't mean that I have to stagnate as a breeder of children in the back of beyond! I'm a business woman, no one knows Mackay Hotels the way I do, and I'll be darned if I let some backwoods——' she paused, biting her lip.

'Backwoods peasant?' he suggested tersely, pulling her to him as he helped her from the car, his eyes a sudden hard black. 'I'm not that, but there's enough pride in me to want to take charge of family affairs, and that happens to include Mackay Hotels. So get used to the idea that I, and not you, will be telephoning David Warner from now on.'

The first of a procession of cars was nosing up

into the forecourt, and Fiona stepped back angrily, her eyes showing more animation than they had for the last two weeks.

'I thought you weren't interested in Mackay money?' she scorned.

'I'm not. But I doubt if James Mackay would have wanted control to go to a man like Warner.'

Fiona stared at him impotently, distracted by the loud cries of greeting that erupted from the arriving cars as if they hadn't seen each other for months instead of the scant minutes between church and Glenappon.

'We'll discuss this later,' she said in a voice more fitted to the boardroom than a dewy-eyed bride, suffering his arm around her waist as they led the way into the ancient hall decorated with flowers from the estate. Wall sconces gleamed against the grey rock with their profusion of gold and yellow flowers, every available table surface proclaimed the spicy harvest of the Glenappon flower beds. Mary and her kitchen staff had been busy for days preparing the food that weighed down tables temporarily placed in the vast hall.

It was like Uncle Fergus's funeral all over again, Fiona thought as she saw the onslaught on the white-clothed trestles. Thick crusted game pie became a staple item on buffet plates, green salad and floury baked potatoes necessary adjuncts. The reason for the feast seemed secondary to the accompaniments to it, and the busy hum of conversation drowned out the gentle notes of the musicians hired for the occasion.

Fiona's smile had once again become stiffly fixed on her face as she accepted the good wishes of those who had been first at the tables.

'You won't go wrong with Roderick, lass,' a

burly, red-faced tenant told her seriously. 'I've known him since he was a boy, and there isn't a better man living.'

'It's really romantic,' one of the maiden Stairs sisters, who rented one of the Glenappon estate cottages, twittered. 'Roderick is such a nice man, so thoughtful. . . .'

'You're a lucky lass,' a stocky farmer-type told her seriously. 'There's not a lot of men like Roderick Cairns left in the world today. I mean, how many young men can you find today who stand by the old rules of gentlemen? He's honest, and upright, and I'd stake my life on his word. Maybe that doesn't mean very much to an American lady like yourself, but. . . .'

'Oh yes, it does,' Fiona assured him, smiling, her eyes reaching to where Roderick was filling plates at the white-clothed buffet. He had been waylaid, she saw, by the languid niece of Lady Carstairs, his head inclined politely towards her as she chatted abstractedly, one eye sweeping across the laden banquet table.

'You must be famished, Fiona,' Isabel said repentantly at her side. 'You didn't have much for breakfast, and . . .'

'Don't fash yourself, Mother,' Roderick loomed at her right hand, his eyes seeking Fiona's with a half-amused glint. 'From now on, it's my job to take care of Fiona's needs. What would you like to eat, darling?'

Fiona's forced smile tightened as she glared at his equally forced endearment. 'Nothing,' she gritted in a low voice so that the anxiously hovering Isabel missed the venom in the single word.

'But you must eat something, sweetheart,' he

protested without similar reticence. 'I'll choose something for you that will bring your appetite back to life.'

'No!' But he had already gone, his dark-clad shoulders easily distinguished at the first of the trestle tables, even among the burly Highland men.

Isabel turned back from a passing greeting to the Sunday-best dressed wife of the tenant farmer who had told her she was a lucky lass. Beaming, she said with satisfaction, 'Roderick is right to see that you eat properly, you have little enough flesh to spare.' Her eye ran appraisingly over Fiona's slenderness, emphasised by the heavy folds of the wedding dress that followed faithfully the swells and indentations of her figure. She sighed, and her eyes grew misty. 'It is indeed a blessing for a woman to have a man to take care of things for her.'

The Women's Liberation Movement could not have pounced more quickly or fiercely on Isabel's innocently worded submission to male dominance than Fiona did; her free-spirited independence of thought and action still smarted under Roderick's high-handed taking over of Mackay Hotels affairs.

'I've never found a man necessary for the decisions I've had to make for the company,' she retorted coolly. 'In fact, I think women are better equipped to deal with problems that arise in the home or in business. They're not sidetracked by dreams of glory that might have applied in the sixteenth century but have no place in today's highly technical world.'

Isabel was obviously embarrassed at her own inability to respond, or even to understand, her new daughter-in-law's hard-edged spate of words.

'Yes ... well, I can only say that I have appreciated the two men I have been married to. I was important to them, and. . . .' she smiled half apologetically, 'I was content with that, though I understand things are different today.'

'They certainly are,' Fiona returned with unbridelike heat. 'Women today are taking their rightful place in the business——'

'Here you are, my love,' Roderick interposed, his blandly fond eyes giving no indication of having heard their conversation. 'There's a little salmon from our Highland streams, a tender breast of grouse from our moorland, and a salad made from potatoes and onions grown in Glenappon's fine soil. Don't be too long about eating it, because we should leave soon, before our guests are too inebriated to wish us well on our honeymoon.'

Fiona automatically curled her fingers round the heavy Glenappon crested plate—the crest appropriately signifying the eagle and the salmon—but her eyes reflected the seething turmoil within her.

'I'm going to phone David,' she insisted glacially, 'he'll be expecting——'

'I talked to him earlier today,' Roderick returned equably, smiling and nodding to a bucolic-looking farmer who passed, looking bewildered, with an overloaded plate.

'You *what*?' Fiona demanded furiously, her own plate wobbling dangerously as she stared disbelievingly at the man who was now her husband . . . her liege lord, entitled to invade every privacy she had held precious until now.

'He extended his best wishes,' he recited as if David were one of the motley crew inhabiting the hall of Glenappon, 'and said to tell you that Mackay, Jamaica, was in the bag, or words to that effect.'

Fiona was instantly transported from the high-ceilinged walls of Glenappon to the torrid lushness of the island Mackay had tried to woo for years.

Eagerly she set aside personal woes to enquire avidly, 'So what did he say? Can we open a Mackay in Jamaica?'

'That seemed to be the gist of his message,' Roderick confirmed with chilling certitude. 'But meanwhile, it's time for you to make the magical transformation into an excited bride throwing her bouquet to the hungry masses of Glenappon maidens.'

Ridiculously, the traditional throwing of the wedding bouquet still made a local maiden a female of prominence in the marriage lottery stakes. Fiona, dressed in a lilac suit of slim-fitting skirt and loose overjacket, tossed the wedding bouquet and felt ironic amusement when Catriona fielded it and clasped the already wilting flowers to her fulsome bosom. The dark eyes avoided Fiona's and concentrated on Roderick's, her expression eloquent of the joys that might have been had another woman, more amply endowed with the worldly goods Glenappon needed, not intervened.

But it was the genuine shouts of goodwill from the guests assembled in the forecourt that echoed in Fiona's mind as Roderick directed the station wagon down and on to the undulating road that set an inexorable course for Edinburgh. Heather sweeping across the hillsides was a purple robe interspersed with burbling streams making their way forcefully to the sea that welcomed their addition to its swollen fulsomeness.

'It's very important to me,' she said in a low voice, 'that Mackay Hotels makes it in the international world. I know it can't mean much to you, but. . . .' she drew a heavy breath, 'it meant a lot to my father.'

Roderick spared a glance for her before turning back to the winding road before them. 'I'm aware of that,' he said tersely. 'I'm aware also that he would have wanted a happy life for his daughter. I can provide that, Fiona, if you give me a free hand to do so.'

Fiona drew a deep breath, leaning back on the headrest as Isabel's pre-liberation words echoed in her mind. 'It is indeed a blessing for a woman to have a man to take care of things for her.' She could accept Roderick's handling of her affairs, or make her own stand against the male dominance of hundreds of years. It would be treacherously easy to accept the lesser role assigned to women in history . . . to yield to greater, and somehow comforting, male certitude. But no one, including Roderick Cairns, knew the intricacies of the Mackay Hotels enterprise as she did. James Mackay's dreams had been fulfilled far beyond his early ambition. His name flared from high-rise hotel buildings from Albuquerque to Zambia. Jamaica was yet another feather in the Mackay bonnet . . . Fiona was determined to fill the gaps that had been left in the world that had become James's oyster. That he had willed her an onerous burden was a fact she had to cope with as best she could.

Her eyes strayed to the countryside her father must have loved; the tumbling streams dividing purple heather hillsides that basked in the warm balm of summer on their steep slopes; the intently cropping sheep finding sustenance on the sparse grasses interwoven with the heather; the rare sight of a farm worker—a shepherd?—discernible on distant moorland.

'My father loved this country,' she said emotionally, bringing a swift glance from Roderick, who guided the station wagon on its relentless way, clinging to the curves, surging with power on the straight stretches. 'I wish he'd been able to come and see it again, just once more.' She paused, choked by sudden tears.

Despite the resentment she still felt at his arrogant statements within minutes of their marriage, Fiona was comforted when Roderick took one hand from the wheel and covered her own, lying loosely on her lap.

'You'll come to love it too,' he said quietly, squeezing her hand before returning his to the wheel. 'Just give it—and me—a chance, Fiona.'

She gave an undignified gulp and blinked the tears from her eyes with a rapid motion as she stared at his strong, calm profile. Nothing ever seemed to disrupt his phlegmatic nature, although it housed so many different aspects. To Isabel, he was a devoted, rather protective, son; with the tenants and estate workers he was a man among men, yet retaining his air of quiet authority; to the few visitors to the new hotel in the past two weeks, he was an affable host, seemingly unaware of their fascination with his looks, his accent, his quietly amused smile. Towards herself he displayed yet another facet of his character; on the surface, he was calmly polite and solicitous of her comfort, but now and then she had surprised a brooding, half-mesmerised look in his eyes across the hearth in the small sitting room. In her numbed state, she had taken those looks as comparisons with the woman he would rather have had sitting opposite him at the cosy fireside. But when she had, piqued by her curiosity, slipped into his room one day while he was out on the estate, the picture of himself and the fair girl had disappeared. . . .

CHAPTER SEVEN

DISPLAYING an unexpected streak of sentimentality, Roderick had chosen the hotel in Edinburgh where they had spent that first night in separate togetherness, for their honeymoon.

But this time there was no barrier of a night table between beds; he had reserved a suite—the honeymoon suite?—that boasted a separate, heavily furnished sitting room as well as a room that seemed to have been built round the huge double bed that took up most of the space, leaving only a little for the antique wardrobe that almost reached the high ceiling.

Following Fiona into the bedroom, having tipped and dismissed the elderly bellboy who had wheezed noticeably as he wheeled their luggage in on a trolley, Roderick said with customary matter-of-factness, 'I've arranged an early dinner for us at a place I think you'll like. Then I have a surprise for you afterwards.'

The surprise of spending her first night in bed with a man? Fiona queried drily, and silently. With his serious outlook on life, intimate jokes were taboo. She didn't care for them herself, she reflected as she went to her suitcase and unzipped it, laying back the lid and exposing the white froth of her nightdress, then closing it again as she turned nervously to face him.

'What kind of thing should I wear?' she frowned with simulated concern, as if the question were a momentous one.

'What?' Roderick stared at her in a way that suggested the intricacies of women's dress escaped him. 'Oh . . .' he pondered, 'something black, you look very good in that. And take something warm for later,' he tossed over his shoulder as he went to the door.

'You're going out?' Fiona raised her brows, piqued yet relieved that he evidently intended to leave her alone to bathe and dress.

Frowning as if irritated at already being asked to account for his movements, he said curtly, 'I've arranged to meet some business associates, but I'll be back in plenty of time to get ready myself.'

Feeling as if she had been projected into a replay of that first night she had spent in Scotland, Fiona went into the bathroom and ran water for her bath into the vast, old-fashioned tub. So why would he waste precious time on a bride he had no option but to marry? Why not have a relaxed drink or two with his cronies before finalising the contract that would bind him to her and Glenappon for all time?

Stepping into the tub, she let her thoughts expand with her limbs. It didn't have to be for all time. All Roderick cared about was for her to produce an heir for Glenappon. Once that was accomplished, she could go back to running the Mackay chain, filling her life as she was used to with the busyness of commerce. She would have fulfilled her part of the bargain.

Meanwhile, he wasn't such a bad bargain as a temporary husband; he was bright, capable, good-looking; she would be envied by most women of her acquaintance ... though she doubted if his quiet doggedness, that stubborn male certainty, would appeal for long to their liberated thinking. Would it bother her? Frowning, she rinsed the thick creamy soap from her arms. Having always been a totally independent woman in her working life, thanks to her father, she had never really dwelt on the politics of the women's movement. Now, she reflected with a dry smile, the question might become more than academic.

Stepping out, she reached for a towel and dismissed the subject from her mind. What did it matter anyway? This promised to be the shortest marriage on record!

Her worries about Roderick walking in while she was dressing hurried her movements, but he still hadn't returned when she fastened on the diamond-circled sapphire earrings that matched the dress she had chosen in preference to the black Roderick had suggested. A small act of defiance to start off the marriage? Punishment for leaving her alone on their wedding evening, making it obvious to his friends that she was unimportant in his scheme of things? Irritably, Fiona shook her head at her reflection in the dresser mirror. Consistency had always been a hallmark of her character; why was she changing now?

Because, she glanced furiously at her watch as she walked into the starchy atmosphere of the sitting room, whatever the business reasons that had taken him out he was unforgivably late. Twitching aside the thick lace panel covering one of the long narrow windows, she stared moodily down into the Georgian square where the hotel entrance was situated. The quiet dignity of the architecturally grand buildings was emphasised by the deserted street and pavements ... did the entire city pack up and go home at six?

About to drop the curtain back in place, her hand checked. A couple emerged from the hotel and stood talking outside, the man's back to her but the blonde woman's face clearly visible as she raised it in what seemed a pleading way to his. A vagrant tingle of envy ran through Fiona as she watched the comforting way the man placed his hands on the woman's shoulders and gripped the navy topcoat she was wearing. The hands were so like Roderick's that for a moment she fantasised that the man was Roderick and that he was holding her shoulders like that, as if he really cared. . . .

He wasn't unlike Roderick in other ways too, she mused, watching idly as the dark head bent to the woman's cheek to kiss her. His hair had the same thick vitality, his head the same shape. Even the suit he was wearing was like the one Roderick had been wearing. . . .

Oh God, it *was* Roderick!

Her hand tightened whitely on the curtain, then let it fall back into place, but she still stood there staring at it in shocked amazement. There had been no mistake. The man had turned to re-enter the hotel while the woman walked off down the street, her head bent low as if she might be crying. His face had been perfectly clear.

Stiffly, Fiona turned and walked to the sofa, which delivered the discomfort it promised in its forbiddingly harsh upholstery. Feeling began to seep back painfully to her numbed senses. It was as if someone had dealt her a body blow, and she folded her arms across her stomach to cradle the pain. The woman hadn't been just any blonde; she was the one in the picture in Roderick's room, the one he had removed recently. Removed her from his dresser, she thought dully, but not from his heart. If ever a man had been emotionally moved by a woman, it was down there on the street minutes ago.

Minutes ago ... Fiona looked at her watch as if she had never seen it before, panicking when she realised that he was probably walking along the hall to their suite at this minute. She couldn't let him see she cared ... or even that she had seen him with the woman.

Anger began to replace shock as she went quickly back into the bedroom, removing her earrings and placing them on the kidney-shaped dressing-table so that she would have something to do with her hands when he came. How dared he insult her by bringing his lover to the very hotel where his new wife awaited him upstairs? It showed a crassness she wouldn't have believed of him ... it also showed that he wasn't now and never could be in love with her, Fiona. Well, she hadn't wanted him to be, had she? Their marriage was unemotionally contracted for unemotional reasons. Only minutes ago she had been comforting herself with the thought that it wouldn't be for ever, she would resume her old life at the earliest opportunity. So why was she acting as if it mattered that he hadn't been able to resist, even on his wedding day, seeing the woman he had been in love with for years?

It was a matter of pride, she told herself stormily. Everyone in the hotel, reception clerks, bellboys, chambermaids, must be snickering at the forlorn bride awaiting the return of her enviably virile husband. The woman herself—had she *pitied* her? That would be the last straw.

Fiona looked at herself in the mirror and saw what she always did—the lively sheen of her red-gold hair drawn back at the sides in a smooth chignon, deep blue eyes intensified by the colour of her expensive and figure-flattering dress, a small straight nose, lips that needed only a light covering of salve to outline their symmetrical fullness.

She was far, far better looking than the blonde Roderick had clung stubbornly to over the years. In fact, the other woman had given off a faint note of shabby gentility, as if her clothes had been styled to wear for ever.

Fiona's fingers tightened on the edge of the dressing-table when she heard Roderick's key in the lock. Dear heaven, don't let me make a fool of myself, let him know I care ... what was she thinking of? Of course she didn't care. Nothing had changed. He was her expedient husband, she was his expedient wife.

Amazingly, he was smiling expansively as he came into the bedroom, his hands already loosening the knot of his tie as he looked approvingly at her appearance.

'I'm sorry, I was held up, but I won't be long. You look beautiful, as always.' He strode across to the massive wardrobe and jerked the door open, his light mood changing to irritation. 'You haven't unpacked yet?'

Of course ... acting the part of dutiful wife while he dallied with his mistress three floors below would have meant that his clothing was arranged neatly in the wardrobe for his selection.

'I've unpacked my own things,' she said coolly, picking up an earring from the dressing-table and glancing at him in the mirror. 'I've left plenty of space for your things in the wardrobe.'

'Most wives attend to their husband's unpacking as well as their own,' he observed tightly, unzipping his battered leather suitcase and scooping up an armful of suits, socks and underwear, dropping several of them as he carried them to the wardrobe.

'I'm not most wives,' Fiona retorted sharply, swinging back to the mirror to deal with the second earring, hearing the clatter of hangers as he hung his suits on them.

'No, you're not,' he agreed softly, savagely, his footsteps muted on the carpet as he came up behind her and turned her forcefully to face him. 'But you're *my* wife, and you'll act accordingly.' His eyes blazed from their craggy depths and Fiona flinched, feeling the hard pressure of his fingers at the soft flesh of her upper arms. Her head reared back defiantly.

'Your wife?' she mocked, 'or Glenappon's?'

For a moment Roderick seemed confused. Then he said roughly, dropping his hands from her, 'They're the same thing, aren't they?' Turning back to the wardrobe, from which he extracted a suit only slightly darker than the one he was wearing, he said tightly, 'I'll be ready in fifteen minutes.'

Fiona watched his striding progress to the bathroom as the mirror reflected it, then went back into the sitting room, resuming her seat at one corner of the unhospitable sofa. What had she expected? Moonlight and roses, sweet talk at her ear? Those were girlhood fantasies; they had no reference to a marriage contracted without love, with no other emotion than expediency involved.

The facts were simple in their clarity. Roderick owned Glenappon by what she would always regard as default. She was the last of the Mackays of Glenappon, the only possible source of Mackay blood to carry on the line. Her father would have wanted it.

Yet another aspect of Roderick's character revealed itself as they ate dinner at a restored historic house turned restaurant. He was apparently a history buff, too.

'John Knox, the religious reformer, was the biggest thorn in Mary, Queen of Scots' side,' he explained over the salty fish offering from the Firth of Forth, the body of water that edged inward from the sea to reach Edinburgh and beyond. 'He made it uncomfortably obvious that he didn't agree with the high-living style of Mary and her courtiers. He was a fanatic Protestant, of course, and Mary was a French Catholic.'

'French?' Fiona went along with his obvious desire to make this a normal wedding dinner. 'I thought she was Queen of Scotland?' She slaked her thirst from the salt-laden fish with several sips of the tart white wine that accompanied their meal.

'She was born in Scotland, but she went to France as a child. She married the Dauphin, but he died before it was consummated.' The word sat easily on his tongue, but Fiona gulped with embarrassing haste on the last of her fish.

'I—always thought she was abducted by the man who became her husband,' she managed with difficulty.

'She was,' Roderick smiled drily, 'but the Earl of Bothwell was her third, not her first, husband.' Absently, he refilled her glass and then his own. 'He was ambitious, and he had no qualms about abducting a queen herself if she could further his cause.'

Nothing in his precise exterior indicated an acknowledgement that he himself was following in the illustrious Earl's footsteps by marrying her and securing Glenappon for himself and his heirs. Fiona wasn't queen of a country, but as head of Mackay Hotels she wasn't without power, influence. Perhaps her nightmare, that first night in Scotland, of being abducted by a man on horseback and spirited through cobbled streets wasn't so far short of the mark after all.

Roderick looked at his watch. 'Unless you particularly want to stay for Edinburgh Pudding and a liqueur that would knock you off your feet, we'll set out now for——'

'I couldn't eat another thing,' Fiona cut in hastily, reaching for her slim purse that matched the black of her shoes. She especially didn't fancy Edinburgh Pudding, which sounded stodgy in the extreme, a dessert not calculated to sit well on her churning stomach.

Yet it was difficult not to relax and enjoy the stirring marches, the precision footwork of the army bands, trained for just such a spectacle as the Edinburgh Tattoo. Roderick had reserved seats with the best possible view of the display, put on every year, he explained, at Festival time. And the Festival, she learned, was a general celebration of the Arts; music, theatre, painting taking place at various areas in the city for two glorious weeks.

Gradually, the image of the blonde woman

faded to manageable proportions. Would Roderick be sitting here with her now, his strong white teeth glinting in the wash of light from the illuminated castle square, if he was secretly yearning for that other woman to be at his side?

'Cold?' he asked when she shivered involuntarily, and quite naturally took her hand in his warm one. 'Enjoying it?'

Fiona nodded, her eyes shining. 'Thanks for thinking of this. I've never felt as Scottish as I do now.' It was true. Her blood had never coursed so proudly as when the kilted drummer had sounded a solitary roll, repeating it into the dramatic silence, despite the crowd, of the Castle ramparts. It was a call to battle in defence of clan and country, and Fiona responded with a pounding pulse, the light in her eye. She must really learn more about her heritage; Roderick would teach her, he knew Scottish history. As another stirring march began, she turned eagerly to him and surprised an odd look in his deepset eyes. It could have been a trick of the fitful light, but she was sure she saw an agonised longing there, as if . . . as if he regretted that Fiona, and not the blonde, was the one whose hand he held.

It must have been her imagination, for his hand pressed hers as he said in a husky voice made almost inaudible by the swell of music, 'How could you have doubted your heritage? You have the wild red hair of the Highlands, and much of their beauty, I. . . .' the rest was finally drowned out, and soon they were filing from the benches and walking across the cobbled courtyard with hundreds of other spectators.

Roderick retained his warm clasp on her hand as they shuffled slowly forward, but Fiona wondered if it was a mechanical thing. He would have been just as courteously attentive had his mother accompanied him ... and more loving with the blonde? The question pursued her down through the stone-canopied exits and to the car he had necessarily parked some distance away. He still kept her hand firmly in his, even when there was no need for it to keep them together.

Somewhere between the castle ramparts and the familiar station wagon a new spirit of competitiveness gripped her. Why should the blonde have things her own way? She might have held Roderick's heart for years, nurtured by stolen weekends from Glenappon or his engineering job, but he had married her, Fiona. The reason was no longer important.

Her sense of euphoria continued after their return to the hotel. Roderick had ordered a late supper to be served in their suite; fruit of the sea again, but this time the sweet flesh of lobster tails smothered in a palate-tingling sauce, tender tips of asparagus, the crisp green of salad. The meal was served on a starched white cloth covering the central table in the sitting room, the waiter withdrawing discreetly after a sleight-of-hand exchange with Roderick.

She didn't need the food, or the wine that Roderick poured into crystal glasses, but she toyed with one and sipped at the other to please him. And strangely, she wanted to please him ... to bring that bemused glow to his eyes, that involuntary huskiness to his voice.

'To us,' he toasted, raising his glass of pale white wine in solemn acknowledgement of the occasion. 'May we have many happy years together.'

Many happy years . . . Fiona's eyes were veiled as she toasted with him their future together. Why did it matter so much that the blonde woman's palely pleading image rose up like a rebuke between them? Like Catriona, she was in love with Roderick . . . probably with more cause. It wasn't hard to imagine his hurried trips to Edinburgh to be with his love, to make love to her. . . .

'I'm really not very hungry,' she disdained the generous helping he heaped on her plate. 'Do you mind if I go and sit down?'

Without waiting for his answer, she pushed her chair back and rose, walking unsteadily to the moralistically upright couch and collapsing on to it. 'I'm sorry,' she murmured as Roderick abandoned his own meal and came to join her, his thigh hard against hers when he sat down on the ungiving sofa.

'Don't be sorry,' he said in a huskily deep voice, his fingers warmly abrasive as they grazed tantalisingly across the soft rise of her cheekbone and down to the vulnerable hollow of her throat where a pulse suddenly began to beat a turgid rhythm. 'You're my wife, my bride, and I would think less of you if you were not a little apprehensive. But I would never hurt you, Fiona,' his voice caressed even as his hands caressed with slow surety the fullness of her breasts, the narrow indentation of her waist, the flare of her hips. Fiona felt as if she were floating on a sea of featherdown, her mouth an alien entity that lifted and met the gentle downward press of his. Her fingers stroked the hard line of his jaw, feeling the sharp rasp of his chin before trailing up across his cheek to the high ridge of bone that helped shroud his deepset eyes. Without seeming volition, her body turned in his arms and pressed itself to his, her breasts suddenly welcoming the half painful pressure of his muscled chest against them.

She couldn't have told how long they lay against the stiff upholstery, or just when Roderick's kisses became harder, fiercer, more demanding of her response. Her sense whirled as unfamiliar sensations welled up inside her and rushed to overwhelm them. Faintly she heard the snatched murmurs of his endearments, the passionate love talk she had never heard before, but seemed to recognise somehow . . . and when Roderick groaned and rose with her in his arms, she made no protest but curled her arms round his neck and returned the kiss that joined them until he laid her gently on the high-lofted bed, his fingers dexterous as he dealt with zippers, hooks, the intricacies of her clothing until she lay exposed to his dark-eyed gaze.

Strangely, she felt no embarrassment in her nakedness. It was as if her body had been made beautiful just for him, and she knew that the soft pink and white of her body excited him as much as her senses were inflamed by the hard bronze of his sinewy flesh when he lay beside her moments later. It was as if all her life had led towards this moment.

'Oh, my darling, my wee wife,' he murmured hotly against her ear, his hands more eloquent than his words as they cupped and stroked and sent shivers of anticipation through her.

He seemed not to be surprised by the harsh cry of pain that escaped her when he took her finally. He had expected a virgin bride, and found her in Fiona. Nothing had prepared her for that exquisite pain, or the euphoric ecstasy that followed. . . .

The voice on the telephone was low and hesitant. 'I'm sorry to trouble you, but is it possible for me to speak to Roderick?'

Fiona was jerked into wakefulness, instinct telling her that the softly cadenced Scottish voice belonged to the blonde woman from Roderick's past.

'I—I'm afraid he's not here right now,' she returned carefully. 'May I take a message for him?'

'Well . . . no, I'll telephone again later.'

The line went dead, and Fiona replaced the receiver thoughtfully. Despite her innocuous voice, the woman had unlimited gall to phone here, where she knew Roderick was honeymooning with his bride!

Honeymooning, she thought, her lips curving into a distracted smile. That was exactly what they had been doing. Days of wandering through city streets drenched with the history Roderick retailed so well, nights when Fiona blossomed gladly into the softer, more sensuous woman she was meant to be under his skilled lovemaking. The other woman had faded into obscurity, and now Fiona resented her re-entry into the private world she had created with Roderick.

Tossing the covers aside, she padded barefoot to where her oyster silk robe lay over a round-backed chair squeezed in between the vast wardrobe and the dresser, fastening it round her as she went into the sitting room. But she already knew that Roderick wouldn't be there . . . his habit was to rise at dawn or shortly after and take himself off on one of the long walks he enjoyed before breakfast.

She was back in the bedroom when she heard

him turn the key in the lock; she flew on bare feet
into the sitting room and met him as he turned
from the door, seeing the smile that instantly lit up
his sombre features when he saw that she was
waiting for him.

'What are you doing up so early?' he asked,
seeming to taste the warmth of her lips as he bent
his head and kissed her, one arm held behind his
back. 'How can I make a surprise for you on your
breakfast tray,' he said huskily, 'if you're already
up and about?' He brought from behind his back a
pale mauve starry flower on a long stalk, and
Fiona's eyes glowed as she took it from him. Every
morning he had brought an offering from his
wanderings; sometimes a blossom he had filched
from some unsuspecting owner's garden, but more
often a wild flower that gained in importance from
its historic site of origin.

Holding the fragile flower to her breast, Fiona
looked up at him and suddenly wished she could
forget the woman who had called. She had never
thought it possible to be this much in love with
another human being. Her eyes hung on every
change in his deepset eyes, every husky cadence in
his voice. She didn't want to think of the woman
who felt confident enough of her hold to telephone
him on his honeymoon. She did want to feel that
she was the only one in the world who knew
intimately the joy of his loving, the pink glow of
health under his tanned cheeks on these mornings
when he returned from his solitary walks, the
sureness of his love for her. At the same time, she
was consumed with curiosity about the woman
who dared call him on his honeymoon.

'There was a call for you,' she said casually,
twisting out of his loose hold and padding over to

the vase already filled with his tokens, tucking the mauve flower in before turning to look at him levelly with her blue eyes.

'Oh? Who was it?'

Roderick pulled down the zipper of his beige jacket as he came further into the room.

'She wouldn't say. She just asked for Roderick, and said she'd call again later when I said you weren't here.'

He shrugged. 'She'll be lucky to find me in later,' he said offhandedly, tugging off the jacket and throwing it on one of the faded side chairs, which looked as if it resented the indignity. 'I'm taking you somewhere entirely different today,' he dismissed the caller with an anticipatory gleam of more immediate pleasure in his eyes.

Each day, he had unfolded a new treasure for her delight. There had been a tour, conducted by himself, of the Castle and its tragic history; an informal walk from there down the Royal Mile to the Palace of Holyroodhouse, its romantic turrets outlined against the bald rise of an undulating hill he called Arthur's Seat.

'I used to slide down that slope on the seat of my pants when I was a boy,' he had reminisced nostalgically, indicating a precipitous rock slide. 'I'm afraid my mother didn't appreciated the wear and tear on my clothes.'

'I can imagine.'

What Fiona couldn't imagine, believe, was her own happiness. Their daily excursions were no different from those of the many tourists who flooded into Edinburgh, but they held a special magic for her. For the first time in her life she felt free to be herself, to enjoy the simple pleasures taken for granted by most people. She drank in avidly the droplets of history that Roderick scattered with knowledgeable certitude, even going so far as to inherit his prejudice against the fearsome John Knox and his bigoted attitude towards Mary, Queen of Scots.

'She came from a light and gay court in France,' he explained pensively as they stood in the small supper room from which her servant, David Rizzio, had been dragged from her skirts and cruelly murdered on the floor below at the instigation of her second husband, the weakly ineffectual Lord Darnley. 'Scotland must have seemed bleak and dour to her, but she never lost her gentle manners, not even when Knox stood before her and denounced her as a harlot.'

It was as if the doomed Mary were still his liege lady, Fiona had reflected drily, but thought at the same time how different Mary's fate would have been had she possessed more stalwart champions like Roderick at the time.

'Do you think she was in love with Lord Bothwell?' she asked pensively, her eyes going round the small supper room and marvelling at its tiny proportions—most American homes boasted a far more luxurious living room.

'Who can tell from this distance?' Roderick shrugged. 'Just the fact that she agreed to marry him means very little. In those days, marriage was the only honourable course for a woman abducted by force, unless she had kinsmen to redress her wrongs.'

So the fated Queen had no choice but to bow to the conventions of her time? The question intrigued Fiona, as did most of her country's history. She was too much a child of the New World to understand the intricacies of the Old.

Yet Roderick had the gift of inspiring an avid interest in the land of her forebears.

What new vistas was he about to unfold this morning? she wondered as she bathed quickly and dressed in the prescribed tweed skirt and sensible brogues she had bought at one of the better stores lining the left side of Princes Street. They had already covered the major historic points of the city itself, and even taken in the Zoo at—where was it?—Corstorphine, and the Botanic Gardens with their natural and exotic flora. They were places she would never normally have time for, but seen through Roderick's proudly nationalistic eyes they took on an enchantment that piqued her curiosity. One day, she had promised herself brightly, she would even learn from him how to pronounce the difficult names peculiar to the Highlands, names that ran so fluently off his tongue.

She came back to the present when a knock sounded at the outer door and moments later Roderick called, 'Breakfast is here, darling.'

'I'll be right there,' she called back, but her fingers stubbornly refused to move the brush she had raised to stroke through the fine red-gold of her hair. Could she really be this much in love with a man she had barely known weeks ago? So much so that his voice seemed to vibrate like a well-known chord along the length of her spine?

David ... poor David ... might never have existed. She had never felt this way for any man, never felt this vitally alive before. But now there was a cloud on her horizon. The light Scottish accent of the blonde woman reverberated in Fiona's ear. Why couldn't she leave Roderick alone? He was married now, whatever his previous romantic commitments had been.

And he loved her, Fiona ... there was no way he could have simulated the passion he overwhelmed her with every night. He was a reserved Scot; he had never actually come out and said that he loved her, but words of love wouldn't come easily to him. His actions spoke for him. Actions that woke the slumbering sensual parts of her nature and drew out the primeval woman so that she responded passionately to his demanding ardour.

Still, uncertainty nagged at her as she went finally into the sitting room and took her place opposite Roderick at the central table. Had he been more offhand than usual after hearing about the woman's telephone call? No, of course not ... he had been as enthusiastic as ever while planning the excursion for today, one of the many he delighted in surprising her with.

But how could she tell? Behind the smile that answered his, her thoughts went on. Her experience lay in the field of business. She would know in a minute if, say, Bradley Stevens was plotting deviously against Mackay Hotels. In the emotional stakes, she was like a babe in arms.

'Roderick, I——' she began, at the same time as the telephone rang with alarming confidence.

'I'll get it.' Roderick dropped the spoon he was about to plunge into the large, brown-shelled egg he liked for breakfast, and Fiona schooled her attention on removing the top from hers.

Should she leave him to take the call privately? But she was his wife, there should be no secrets between them. Pinned to the spot by her uncertainty, she went on eating the breakfast that had suddenly lost its flavour for her. Impossible not to hear Roderick's opening words.

'Oh, it's you, Jean,' he said pleasantly. 'Hold on a minute, will you?' Cupping the receiver with his hand, he directed his voice to Fiona. 'Will you mind if I take this in the bedroom? It's—well, it's private.'

Fiona's heart turned over in a sickening way, and she felt the blood drain from her cheeks. But she summoned indifferent coolness as she reached for another piece of toast from the silver rack.

'Not at all,' she dismissed pleasantly, but the toast dropped to her plate as Roderick put down the receiver in an open position and went into the bedroom, closing the door firmly behind him.

Fiona's fists balled into white gloves of fury. How dared he do this to her? Whatever the customs were in Scotland about wives and mistresses, she wasn't about to condone the mingling of one with the other like this. She lifted the bloodless knuckles of one hand and gnawed on them furiously.

What a fool she had been to succumb to his skilled passion! A fool not to confront him about the woman he had kissed so tenderly that first night of their honeymoon. A fool not to question him before falling irrevocably in love with him. Her head lifted.

Irrevocably? Nothing was unchangeable, not even the state of her emotions—particularly the state of her emotions! She could fall out of love as fast as she had fallen into it. Roderick had manipulated her with the expertness of his lovemaking—and why wouldn't he be an expert after all those amorous years with his Jean behind him? Jean! Didn't the other woman in the case always have a name like Tania, or—or Dolores? Exotic names to excite a man's imagination. But

Jean! It was a name for a steadfast wife, a woman who would quietly welcome her husband home at the end of a day's toil.

Why hadn't he married his Jean years ago, she wondered furiously, if he was so much in love with her? Oh, how she wished he had!—that she had never met him except as the unimportant stepson of her Uncle Fergus. But that would have meant, the thought ran on sourly, that the blonde Jean would have been mistress of Glenappon as well as—

'Sorry about that,' Roderick said briskly as he came back into the room and replaced the extension before sitting down to resume his breakfast. There was a deep glow of satisfaction in his warm brown eyes and Fiona diverted her own from it.

What mysterious power did the unexciting Jean hold over him? Whatever it was, Fiona wasn't going to betray her own seething anger by making a scene that would perhaps add to that satisfaction.

'It's all right.' Fiona pushed away from the table. 'I'll go and get ready.'

'But you haven't finished your breakfast.'

She resorted to a slightly pointed dry humour. 'Your Scottish women might have figures that can take unlimited food, but mine can't!'

His eyes went swiftly over the svelte lines of her streamlined body. 'What nonsense. You're just right as you are.'

'And I want to keep it that way,' she retorted lightly, walking towards the bedroom, then turning round, a small frown between her faintly marked brows. 'Would you hate me if I got fat, Roderick?'

He abandoned his napkin and came to her. 'I might object if you turned out like old Mrs Stewart at Glenappon who's so big she spends most of her life in a chair in her cottage kitchen, but I could never hate you, Fiona.' The dancing gleam darkened in his eyes as he reached out his arms and pulled her to the hard length of his body. 'You're all I expected of my wife, and much more,' he said huskily, his warm lips distractingly nuzzling her ear. 'I'm the luckiest man on earth.'

Lucky . . . yes, he was that. Fiona fought against the rising tide of response these past days had made almost automatic. She had proved amenable to the advances she now knew were calculated. Wasn't it a lucky man who had both moneyed wife and a mistress ready, like puppets, to jump when he pulled their individual strings?

She pushed lightly at his chest, feeling the quickened beat of his heart under her palm and suddenly nauseated by it. 'I really can't wait to know what you've planned for today,' she forced lightness, 'and I'm puzzled as to why you told me to wear a warm skirt and these awful shoes.' She looked down at the heavy brogues as she stepped adeptly back, her eyes missing the neat curve of her ankles and seeing only the serviceable ugliness of her footwear. 'Finish your breakfast, and then you'll find out.'

Her mouth held a smile until she escaped into the bedroom, but then her lips firmed to suppress their trembling as she stood before the dressing-table mirror to apply a new film of pale gloss that outlined without emphasising their full curves. They needed no emphasis. Her mouth had become fuller during these past few days—nights!—of a man's passionate love. Love! Roderick loved only two things in life.

Glenappon—and Jean.

CHAPTER EIGHT

RODERICK'S surprise for the day consisted of a tramp over the Braid Hills, slightly south of Edinburgh, hence his instruction to wear sensible clothes.

In other circumstances, it would have been an ideal day . . . the sun shone from a clear blue sky, and the air smelled of gorse and grass with a faint hint of the sea. It hadn't the incredible qualities of Highland air with its mixture of peat and heather and another undefinable quality, but it filled the lungs with its purity as they tramped across the low hills.

Roderick, unusually silent, gave Fiona free rein of her own thoughts. Every one of them seemed bitter. Uppermost was her own chagrin at having been taken for a naïve fool. Had he and Jean sniggered over her gullible submission to Roderick's lovemaking? Made plans for the life of ease he would provide for Jean with Mackay money? No ring on her finger, Fiona reflected bitterly, but soft-toned bells on her toes! Oh, how could she have been so foolish as to think his murmured words of love were sincere?

Even now, his child could be forming inside her, the child he had married her for in his fanatic desire for a continuity of Mackays at Glenappon. But that could be her bargaining point when the final part of this farce came to pass. She would hold the whip hand. The child would be hers, Glenappon nothing without it. Roderick would have no choice but to relinquish his claim on her ancestral home. Oh, she would be reasonably generous when she bought Glenappon from him, and he and his Jean could live in reasonable comfort, but Glenappon would be hers. . . .

'Should we stop here for lunch?' Roderick interrupted her thoughts, indicating a high knoll that took in the swooping spread of green towards the city. Obviously expecting no objection, he unslung the picnic hamper from his shoulder and dropped it on the springy turf.

The hotel had done them proud with seasoned chicken, crisp green salad, and featherlight rolls to form the first course, a container of thick farm cream to accompany the wedges of spiced apple pie for dessert. A bottle of expensive white wine completed the meal, but Fiona drank little of it. Her battered ego needed more than the elusive bubbles of an imported wine to restore its confidence.

'It would be a pity if all this is turned over to the housing developers,' Roderick indicated the fine green slopes leading gently to the environs of the city. 'So little of our heritage is kept for future generations.' He laid aside the chicken leg he had been gnawing on and reached out an arm to draw Fiona to his side. 'But at least we can preserve Glenappon from that kind of development, can't we?' he said, huskily emotional.

Fiona saw her chance and took it. 'We can try, I suppose,' she said in a hard voice that brought his eyes sharply round to her perfectly chiselled profile. 'But you've already started the destruction there, haven't you?' She pulled away from his familiar hold at her waist. 'One thing leads to another—first a hotel, then the side attractions so that guests have something to do apart from drinking in the scenery. It's just one small step from a golf course to a quick food outlet to a popcorn vendor's shack. Is that what you're planning for Glenappon?'

She felt his hard stare, but kept her head averted.

'You know that isn't what I want for Glenappon,' he said in a low voice. His hand reached out and dragged her chin round so that his eyes met hers. 'What's wrong, Fiona?' he asked quietly. 'You haven't been yourself all day. Did I do something to annoy you?'

She shook his hand off and looked at him with scornful blue eyes. 'You haven't the power to annoy me,' she said with brisk arrogance. 'I'm concerned for Glenappon, that's all. I don't think it should be a hotel; it should be kept as a family home. *My* family's home,' she stressed, gaining confidence from the stricken look in his eyes. 'I have more than enough money to make that possible.'

She heard his quick indraw of breath.

'Glenappon is mine,' he said levelly then, 'and I'm not interested in an outpouring of Mackay money. The people there need to take pride in working to a purpose, not growing fat on money they haven't earned by honest labour.'

'Oh, they won't do that,' she shot back, 'because I'll——' She paused and bit her lip, her own thoughts running ahead of caution.

'You'll—what?'

She blinked as she turned the cool blue of her eyes on him and saw the tight clamping of his jaw that spoke eloquently of the anger brimming inside him.

'Technically,' she allowed coldly, 'Glenappon belongs to you, but by every right of inheritance it's mine. Name your price, Roderick, and it's yours. Isabel won't suffer; she can have any home she wants, and you ... you can marry the woman of your choice and never be concerned with money again.'

The muscle at his jaw tensed several times before he forced out harshly, 'You seem to forget that I *am* married, and to the woman I thought was my choice. The mistake was mine.'

He rose violently, leaving her to hastily gather up the remnants of their lunch and stuff them into the basket before following his lengthy stride down the green slope. Tears gathered in an intolerable ache in Fiona's throat as she stumbled after him to where they had parked the wagon. If by the merest chance he had truly loved her, wouldn't he have protested that love back there on the hill? Begged, pleaded with her to remember that love they had shared briefly? No; Glenappon was uppermost in his mind. The wife of his choice had been the one who could deliver Glenappon from the ignominy of obscurity in the Cairns name.

Glenappon received them back royally. Faces Fiona was beginning to recognise as those of tenant farmers and their shyly smiling wives, the few servants who kept the house and gardens, and others she had seen only in passing, lined the entrance to the ancient castle, which basked in the mellow glow of the early autumn sun.

Sharp eyes were keen to note the changes her new status had brought to her, and Fiona didn't disappoint them. Her child, the one she probably carried in her, would appreciate the effort she made now. He or she would learn of the pleased smiles of the Glenappon people, their warm good wishes, on their mother's return from a honeymoon with a man who had served his purpose. There must be some way that the Cairns part of their heritage could be expunged.

Roderick's arm was like a band of steel round her waist as they stood together on the worn flags of the entrance to Glenappon Castle, and she forced a smile to her frozen lips as she leaned against her husband's stalwart figure. They had made a bargain, and she was determined to keep it. Glenappon for an initial show of marital harmony.

The gathering on the following evening had been arranged since the day of their wedding. Roderick had explained tersely that the social occasion was traditional, when the newly married couple was welcomed back by the friends and tenants of the estate farms. Everyone knew that James Mackay's business interests elsewhere were now Fiona's. It would excite no comment when she was called away to deal with an emergency situation in New York . . . her protracted return to Glenappon would excite little comment, and gradually the people would accept that the marriage was over almost before it had begun.

'Welcome home,' Isabel said emotionally, embracing each of them in turn on the wide flagged entrance to the Castle. To Roderick, she said anxiously, 'I think they expect a few words, Roderick.'

Nodding, he turned and faced the congregation of Glenappon residents. Faces turned expectantly towards him.

'We thank you for coming to welcome us home,'

he said in a strong voice, his fingers digging into Fiona's waist, 'and you're all invited to the gathering tomorrow night. I can promise you that not one of you will ever forget the celebrations for the marriage of Fiona Mackay to Roderick Cairns!'

Shouts of approval were still echoing in their ears when Roderick ushered Fiona into the castle hall after his mother. His jovial expression changed to one of intense weariness as he addressed his mother tersely.

'Is everything arranged?'

'Yes,' Isabel returned jerkily, her eyes on the deadly serious cast of her son's. 'I've ordered the musicians, and Maggie has been busy for days cooking and baking. But if you think——'

'No,' he cut in brusquely, the hand he had seemingly forgotten until now dropping away from Fiona's waist, 'Maggie knows what's necessary, but maybe I'd better see if we have enough drink in stock.'

Both women's eyes followed his swift stride across the hall.

'He must be tired after driving all that way,' Isabel stated her opinion nervously, 'although he usually enjoys driving.' She caught herself up and turned to Fiona, smiling. 'You must be tired too, my dear. Your room is all ready, and if you would like to rest for a while I'll send Rena up with some tea in an hour or so.'

Fiona forced a smile. 'Thanks. I—yes, that sounds nice.' She had almost forgotten that Glenappon was now a hotel until the small reception desk caught her eye as she walked across the hall. There was no sign of Catriona behind or around it, and she breathed a sigh of relief that this was obviously the other girl's time off from her reception duties. The dark girl's venom would have been too much to take right now.

Hotel guests, too, were out at this time of day, and she met no one as she mounted the stairs and automatically turned right to go to her old room before remembering that Isabel had likely referred to the suite she and Roderick would now be sharing.

Roderick! He hadn't been tired from driving, but how could she have explained to Isabel that the marriage she and all of Glenappon held high hopes for was already finished? That she, Fiona, would be leaving for New York within the next few days, never to return until. . . .

Steeling her heart, she let her eyes glance round the small private sitting room with its view over the loch and the hills beyond. This led to the larger room where a vast canopied bed held pride of place amidst a priceless collection of antique dressers and wardrobes, all polished to a deep, rich patina. Roderick's handiwork was noticeable everywhere . . . in the newly decorated walls of pale peach with rich cream contrast; in the padded seats underlining the long diamond-paned windows; in the completely reconstructed bathroom where he had installed every convenient gadget known to modern man.

All for her? Or had he had his Jean in mind when he spent his free hours working in here? Her mouth clamped down to stem the tears that rose irritatingly in her eyes, and she walked quickly back into the sitting room with its Wedgwood blue inserts in walls of pristine white forming a background to the blue and white scroll of the upholstery on couches and chairs and on the chaise-longue that was placed to take full advantage of the loch view.

She couldn't stay here with him, sleep in that bed with him, not even for one night, knowing that he would lie awake but unmoving beside her, as he had last night in Edinburgh. Nothing about these rooms he had lovingly formed would prevent the craving to love passionately ... how soon she had become addicted to his ability to arouse desires she had never known existed! He had made it seem so natural, so beautiful. ...

Strangling a sob, she picked up her handbag as she ran from the suite and sought the sanctuary of the room where she had been herself, divorced from the sickening needs of that addiction. Her feet flew along the corridor as if snapping hounds yelped at her heels, and she drew to a halt and stared stupefied at the door of her old room when it refused to open.

'Pardon me, ma'am,' a soft American voice said behind her, 'but I think you have the wrong room. What's your number?'

Her number? Whirling, Fiona stared numbly at the solicitous expression on a pink and plump middle-aged face.

'I—er—yes, I think I do have the wrong room,' she stammered, walking rapidly away until the American called concernedly after her.

'Say, you're from the States, aren't you?'

'Yes.' She turned distractedly back and gestured to the door that was now his. 'I'm sorry about that.'

'No problem,' he said genially, coming towards her. 'These castles are really something, aren't they? When our travel agent suggested we come here I must admit I wondered about the plumbing and that kind of thing, you know? But once we were here, that didn't seem to matter.' He waved a hand that encompassed the dark-visaged portraits lining the wood-panelled passage. 'This is the kind of history my wife, Verna, goes crazy about—and you couldn't have it more authentic. Did you know that there's going to be a shindig here tomorrow night for the present Laird and his new wife? And she's an American,' he added with patriotic awe.

'Yes, I—I heard something about it,' Fiona returned awkwardly, her escape blocked off by the squat figure that planted itself confidently before her.

'Of course, it doesn't need a wizard with a stick,' he went on, his eyes going appraisingly over the seedy-looking wood panelling, 'to know that good old American know-how—and money!— could make a world of difference to this place.' He laughed. 'But from what I hear, this Roderick Cairns has made a good deal for himself. His new wife is the owner of the Mackay Hotel chain—you've heard of them?— and she's not only. . . .'

'Please excuse me,' Fiona interrupted hurriedly, giving her compatriot a nervous smile as she stepped past him. 'I'm sure my room is along this way.'

Ignoring his puzzled frown, she stepped briskly away from him and finally gained what had become the sanctuary of the suite. Closing the cream panels behind her, she leaned back on them momentarily. She had stupidly forgotten that her old room had been rented out to an American . . . probably the rest of the habitable rooms were similarly unavailable. But she couldn't spend this night or any other with Roderick in the same bed as herself.

Her eyes sought the restful beauty of the loch and its sweep of silver-barked birch lining its far shore as she sank on to the chaise-longue, its downy cushions forming a cradle for her emotionally battered frame. How could she have let herself be caught up in that vortex of feeling that would always have bitterness as its base? Slow tears squeezed between her eyes as she laid her head back on the padded headrest.

Too many new emotions had swayed her during the past few days. From a coolly calculating woman of business she had become the pliable tool of the man who had wooed and won her with his expertise in bed. To her, love was new; to him it was a means to an end. And that end was Glenappon. The only thing she didn't doubt about him was his love for this pine-circled estate nestled in the Highlands among the heather and dark green firs. To preserve its long history of Mackay occupation, Roderick had disdained the woman he loved and married another more fit to provide the necessities Glenappon needed. . . .

The rattle of china close to her head brought Fiona out of a dream-filled sleep. Roderick had been bringing her flowers that bloomed profusely beside the loch, and he ran lightly in the way of dreams to toss the pale lilac blossoms at her feet.

'Thank you, Rena,' she said dazedly, recalling Isabel's promise to send the maid up with tea for her. 'I must have fallen asleep. . . .' Struggling to one elbow, she focussed on Roderick's stiffly erect figure disappearing into the bedroom beyond. A slight drop of her eyes told her that he had moved the long and low casual table within close reach of the couch she lay on. Frozenly, she poured the pale amber liquid into the readied cup, her ears alert for the slightest sound from the room beyond.

The tea was piping hot, but she gulped it down to relieve the parched dryness of her throat. She set the empty cup back on its saucer when Roderick came grimly back into the sitting room, his eyes watching hers as they went to the valise in his hand.

'I'll sleep in my own room,' he said shortly. 'Have you made arrangements for your flight to New York?'

'No, I—no, I haven't.' In spite of her competence in other areas, the thought of making her own travel arrangements left her momentarily at a loss. Someone else had always done it for her.

'I'll see to it, if you tell me when you want to go.' His tone indicated only too clearly that her departure couldn't be soon enough for him. It was as if those days, those nights, had never been. A gust of feeling swept over her, regret mixed with anger, leaving a tremble in her voice.

'No, I'd better do it myself. I'll call—David, make it appear as if I'm needed back there.' She would always be needed *there*. . . .

Roderick gave her a curt nod. 'As you wish.'

Fiona struggled to a more upright position as he stalked to the door without another word, her stomach churning with the memory of those well-shaped lips pressed hotly to hers, his lean body ardent with the same desire he had inspired in her. If only he had stopped and said something like, 'You're sure this is what you want?' instead of accepting her decision coldly as he had, she might have weakened.

Or would she? Swinging her feet to the softly carpeted floor, she pushed the low table and its contents away and rose to pace across the room and back again to the window. More than anything, he had hurt her pride, the fierce Scottish pride she had inherited from her father. A bitter smile curled her lips as her eyes wandered vacantly across the still waters of the loch. She, who had so easily seen through the flimsy motives of other men, had been completely taken in by a man whose stakes in gaining her love were so much greater.

Her blue eyes hardened to a marble-like glitter. He thought he could get by without the support of Mackay Hotels—well, let him try. In her heart she had always known he was as averse to seeing 'A Pillow Talk Hotel' emblazoned on the ancient stonework of the Castle as she herself was. He would try to go it alone, with the aid of his Jean, struggling to support the estate from the comparatively small returns of a hotel which, in its present state, was woefully inadequate to do that, let alone modernise the other rooms that might have made it a viable proposition.

No, let them struggle ... sooner or later they would be more than willing to sell Glenappon to her at a price she would set. Passionately, Fiona hoped that a child was forming under her heart. She would restore Glenappon to its rightful state and better; together with her son or daughter she would make it the ancestral home it was meant to be. And the name would be Mackay.

Men, or one special man, played no part in her fantasy of the future. She had had enough of their self-seeking ways.

'So you're back?' Catriona greeted her insolently as Fiona stepped down into the hall later. The red sweater-dress the dark girl was wearing set off her dark hair attractively; in fact, her figure having fined down considerably recently, she was a striking-looking woman. Apart from the malevolent eyes that roamed in slighting appraisal over Fiona's simply styled royal blue dress, she exuded an air of cordial warmth that was so invaluable in the hotel reception world. 'I must say, neither of you seems to have enjoyed the honeymoon very much,' she went on with a sourly pleased smile. 'Roderick has a frown on him like a thundercloud over Ben Lawers, and you don't look much better.'

Fiona gave her a level look that sparked fire although her voice was cool. 'I don't think that's any of your business, as an employee of the hotel.'

An ugly redness spread over the dark girl's skin. 'Don't you talk to me like that!' she spat venomously, her eyes contemptuous as they went again over Fiona's demurely styled, but very expensive, dress. 'Roderick only married you because you had money! Why else would he take a cold fish like you? It's no wonder he's wearing a frown if you treated him like an iceberg on his honeymoon as you did before you were married! A man needs more than money to warm his bed, you know!'

Fiona had never been inclined towards violence, but her palm itched now to slap the other girl's mocking face. Where there had been the murmur of voices and the chinking of dishes from the dining room where the hotel guests ate, there was now a listening silence.

'Now look here, young lady,' a distinctive

American male voice spoke up from behind Fiona, 'you've no right to speak to a guest of the hotel that way!'

Fiona swung round, her face pale, and recognised the man she had encountered outside the door of her old room. 'It's all right, really. I'm——'

'She's not a guest,' Catriona cut in scornfully, 'she's——'

'What in heaven's name is going on out here?' another voice, sternly chill, broke in. Roderick, his face almost as pale as Fiona's, looked exasperatedly from one to the other of them. Fiona noticed that he had changed into the darkest of his suits, which made him look even more formidable.

'The clerk here,' the American blustered irately, 'was being very rude to this little lady, and that's something I can't take. After all, this is a hotel, and you don't expect the guests to be treated like——'

'The little lady,' Roderick sliced with curt sarcasm, 'is not a guest of the hotel, Mr——?'

'Van Pelt,' the other man returned irritably, 'and what do you mean, she's not a guest in the hotel? Just this afternoon she mistook my room for her own!'

Roderick shot Fiona a sharp look, then turned back to the irate American. 'My name is Roderick Cairns, Mr van Pelt, and this is—my wife, Fiona.' The slight pause before the introduction unexpectedly cut through Fiona like a knife.

The American's pink cheeks sagged in puzzled disbelief as he stared at Fiona. 'You're——? But why didn't you say so this afternoon? You must have thought I was a real idiot, Mrs Cairns,' he went on, embarrassed, 'talking about your party tomorrow night as if you didn't know about it.'

'No, of course I didn't, I just——' Fiona found her voice, her eyes flicking to Roderick's flintlike stare. 'I was in a hurry this afternoon to ... to. ...'

'You sure were that,' he chuckled, giving Roderick a man-to-man wink, 'and that's no surprise, considering you just got back from your honeymoon. Please permit me to extend my very best wishes to you both, and I know my wife will——'

'Thank you very much,' Roderick cut him off smoothly, taking Fiona's arm. 'Come along, darling, we've been waiting dinner for you.'

With a faint smile in van Pelt's direction, she allowed him to draw her across the hall to the small sitting room which now doubled as the family dining room at Roderick's insistence that they preserve a semblance of privacy in the hotel setting.

'What was that all about with Catriona?' he muttered furiously, his temper obviously not at its sweetest.

'It was just a misunderstanding,' Fiona soothed quietly, deciding that no purpose would be served in telling him just what Catriona had shouted. He would probably fire the girl, and it would be difficult to replace her with anyone suitable from the estate. 'She—er—just thought it was time she had a break for her meal,' she improvised as he opened the sitting door and stood back for her to enter.

He was frowning as he came to stand level with her. 'She's already had her dinner break,' he said brusquely, though his eyes were searching as they met Fiona's.

'Was something the matter?' Isabel asked,

worried, as they went together towards the round table placed before a window that was now fully curtained against the night coolness. A cheerful blaze in the brick-fronted fireplace made the room a cosily welcoming picture.

Seemingly taking his cue from Fiona, Roderick said as he held her chair for her, 'A storm in a teacup, Mother. One of the American guests thought Fiona needed rescuing from Catriona's sharp tongue—which, by the way, she will have to curb if she wants to go on working here. She can't behave as if she's in her father's kitchen.'

'Oh dear,' Isabel fretted, 'I don't want the guests to be upset—which one was it?'

'His name is van Pelt,' her son stated shortly, helping himself generously from the arrayed dishes, his appetite obviously unimpaired, Fiona noted with a flare of irritation.

'Van Pelt? Oh yes.' Isabel turned to Fiona with a delighted smile. 'He and his wife are in your old room, Fiona, and their two children are next door. This is the second week of their visit, and they certainly seem to be enjoying themselves in the Highlands.'

Roderick's deepset eyes glanced thoughtfully into Fiona's as she murmured a reply. It was as if he guessed that she had fled in panic from the suite he had refurbished with his own hands for his bride. But apart from a tightening of his full-shaped mouth, he made no further comment.

'I'm wondering, Roderick,' Isabel said absently, 'if it might be better to use the hall for a dining room and have the dancing in the drawing room tomorrow night?'

He shrugged indifferently, applying himself to his meal. 'Whatever you like.'

'Heavens, it's not what *I* like!' She glanced at her new daughter-in-law. 'It's what you and Fiona would like that matters.'

'All right then.' He put down his knife and fork and looked with exaggerated interest at Fiona. 'How would you like the gathering arranged?'

She started nervously, spilling several drops of her wine which spread to form a dark red stain across the white cloth. 'Oh, I'm sorry!' she jumped up and dabbed at it with her napkin, pale colour rushing into her cheeks to replace the pallor.

'Och, don't worry about it,' Isabel dismissed, waving her back to her seat. 'It can be soaked as soon as we've finished the meal. Now, Fiona, what do you think of having the dancing in the drawing room?'

'That sounds—just fine to me.' Fiona wondered how she would ever get through the next few days. Surely Isabel—sweet, trusting Isabel—should know the truth about her son's fiasco of a marriage before the whole world did. 'Isabel, I——'

'Oh, by the way, Mother,' Roderick cut in as if sensing what she was about to say, 'I've asked Jean up for the gathering.'

'*Jean?*' his mother asked sharply, her eyes sliding nervously to Fiona before going accusingly back to her son's. 'And just when did you see her?' She said the 'her' as if it left a bad taste in her mouth.

He lifted his shoulders in a shrug. 'In Edinburgh. She hasn't had it easy, Mother,' he added quietly.

The older woman snorted disgustedly. 'What did she expect when she up and left her husband?

I don't hold with divorce, Roderick, as you know.'

'Whether you agree with it or not, it happens,' he said bluntly, looking at neither woman. 'She wasn't happy with Andrew, so she did the only sensible thing.'

Fiona pushed her chair back so violently that her wine was threatened again. Rising, she said to no one in particular, 'If you'll excuse me, I'd like to call David in New York ... just check that everything is all right.'

'Of course, my dear,' Isabel looked startled by her sudden movement, 'but I wish you would finish your dinner first. Anyway, she smiled, 'this David of yours sounds a very competent young man to take care of your affairs.'

'Oh, he is,' Fiona agreed hastily, 'it's just that I'd like to hear it from him direct.' Although she avoided Roderick's eyes on the way past him, they burned twin holes in the back of her blue linen dress until she reached the door. Outside, she bent over as if from a stomach ache, her arms clasped convulsively in front of her.

It was painfully obvious now why Jean hadn't married Roderick years ago. She had been married to someone else ... a man she must have imagined she preferred to Roderick, only later finding out her mistake. No wonder she had looked so distraught that evening on the pavement outside the hotel! To go through the trauma of divorce only to find that the man she really loved had just married someone else! Or had there been a conspiracy between them from the first, with Jean content to take the crumbs of his attention as long as his ambitions for Glenappon were fulfilled? Did she know now that the marriage was over? Those mornings in Edinburgh when she had thought Roderick was walking for his health, had he secretly been meeting the blonde woman?

Her head felt as if it would burst with all the new conjectures swirling around in it, and she pressed her hands to her temples, only re-membering Catriona's vengeful presence when the other girl coughed loudly from the other side of the hall.

Her eyes went to the telephone under the stairs, an ache of loneliness rising in her throat. It would be so good to hear David's voice again, a soothing return to the past which she had never regarded then as being tranquil. She reached him at the office, sudden tears leaping into her eyes when she heard the familiar friendly voice, so schooled in marketing diplomacy.

'Fiona? You must be a mind-reader! I was going to call you tonight and tell you my news. But first, how's the new bride?'

'Just fine, David.' Was his tone just a little too hearty, conveying what he thought she wanted to hear? Had it really upset him so much that she had married the taciturn Scot and left him to cope with Mackay affairs on his own? 'What news are you talking about? Is something wrong?'

'Not a thing,' he returned cheerfully, 'every-thing's going fine in every way.' He chuckled as if he were in the room with her. 'You seem to be setting a fashion, Fiona—guess what? I'm getting married three weeks from now!'

Fiona's hand tightened on the receiver and she turned her back to the openly inquisitive Catriona. Her mind went blank, and then raced. Later she would wonder if David was marrying on the rebound—when had he had time to romance a woman to the point of marriage?—but now she had to think of her own survival. It didn't matter that David would think she had gone mad, she could explain things when she got there.

'Oh, I'm sorry to hear that,' she forced out, loudly enough for Catriona to hear. 'I'll come back right away.'

'Fiona?' David's voice came back understandably puzzled. 'We must have our lines crossed . . . I said I'm getting married in three weeks' time.'

'Three weeks? That's not much time . . . I'll take the first available flight . . . I'll let you know when I'm arriving and we can discuss it on the way from the airport. Goodbye, David.'

She put down the receiver while David was still shouting an exasperated, 'Fiona!' and ignored Catriona as she retraced her steps to the sitting room.

'I'm sorry,' she looked coolly at Isabel as she resumed her chair, 'but I have to rush back to New York. There's a problem David can't deal with.'

'Oh, I'm so sorry,' Isabel sympathised, turning immediately to Roderick, who was staring fixedly at Fiona. 'You'll go with Fiona, of course,' she said with an air of being at her best in a crisis.

'No,' he said slowly at last, 'if she goes, she goes alone.'

His mother stared at him aghast. 'But you're her husband, it's your place to take the worries of business from her shoulders. Of course you'll go!'

Still he kept his gaze fixedly on Fiona's, as if they were frozen into that exchange of glances . . . as if he were aware of the the heavy, sick beat of her heart under the sober royal blue of her high-necked dress.

'Fiona knows more about managing Mackay business than I ever will,' he said flatly. 'It's up to her to choose.'

'I've never heard of such a thing!' Isabel cried, her cheeks a mottled pink, obviously affronted at her son's departure from the mores she had abided by all her life.

'It's between Fiona and me, Mother,' he rebuked sharply, drawing his eyes from Fiona's to give her a coldly significant look that brought her agitatedly to her feet.

'I'm sorry,' she said stiffly, 'I don't mean to interfere. I'll tell Rena to bring your coffee on my way up to my room.'

'Oh, please. . . .' Fiona protested, filled with embarrassment.

'There's no need to get on your high horse, Mother,' Roderick flung at her with scathing impatience.

'I'm not on my high horse,' she returned, dignified as she moved to the door. 'I'm leaving because this is something the two of you have to settle between yourselves. Goodnight to you both.'

A silence filled the room when she had gone, and Fiona wondered if she had sensed, guessed, that the marriage was ending almost before it had begun.

Roderick's expression was hard to read as he lifted the wine bottle and refilled their glasses. He seemed morosely distracted as he drank from his immediately, not noticing if Fiona did the same. This was yet another Roderick, broodily silent with his own thoughts, hinting at the dark and fitful moodiness of his race. The quiet strength of him seemed menacingly contained as his long, competent fingers curled round the rounded crystal of the glass.

Shouldn't he be pleased that she had broken the ice of their impending break-up to his mother, saving her the slow realisation that her son's wife never would come back after her hurried trip to New York? The silence grew more oppressive, and Fiona cleared her throat to say the first thing that came into her mind.

'If you need financial help in getting the hotel established——' she began, flinching when his fist crashed down on the table with a resounding thud.

'Glenappon will survive without Mackay money,' he said thickly, and Fiona glanced at his lowering features with surprise, her eyes then dropping to the glass he still clenched in his fist. His habits had struck her as tending towards the abstemious rather than the opposite, but now it appeared he had drunk deeply of the potent wine ... and who knew how much of his country's mind-boggling spirits before dinner?

'Was he pleased to hear that you're going back to him?' he shot at her so suddenly that she started and blinked as she stared uncomprehendingly across the table.

'What?'

'Your fancy boy-friend,' he slurred contemptuously, 'the one who knows what kind of perfume you use. Although,' he chuckled with sombre humour, 'I doubt if he'd know what to do with a woman if he had her in his bed.'

'David is a—a fine man,' Fiona defended hotly, watching as Roderick got to his feet and stepped with less than his usual grace to the small cupboard behind the door and poured himself a generous measure of brandy.

'A fine man,' he mimicked, coming back to the table and glaring down at her with scathing sarcasm. 'And I suppose he screwed up his courage and asked you to marry him when you're free of me?'

'He talked about marriage, yes,' Fiona agreed, not untruthfully. Sickened by the exchange, she pushed back her chair and rose. 'If you'll excuse me, I think I'll——'

Drunk or not, Roderick moved agilely to intercept her as she started towards the door. His dark eyes held the glitter of the madness she had suspected in him once before as he clamped a steely arm round her waist and dragged her with breath-robbing force against him, hurting her with the pressure of his lean fingers where they dug into her ribcage.

'He talked about marriage, did he?' The demand was savage, his dark features twisted into an unrecognisable pattern as his mouth swooped and hovered over hers. 'Well, maybe I should give you a basis of comparison between your first and second husbands!' His mouth fell hotly on the shocked parting of her lips, forcing them painfully apart, thrusting aggressively where once he had wooed her with gently sensuous persuasion. It was a brutal assault on her senses, and Fiona drew back, gasping.

'Roderick, don't . . . please don't! This isn't like you. . . .'

'How the hell would you know what I'm like?' he snarled fiercely, his fingers tangling in the hair she had arranged in a tight chignon, loosening it so that it fell in a mass to her shoulders. 'You're not staying around long enough to find out, are you? What I can't understand,' his voice dropped to a quieter, more calculating note, 'is why you married me at all, why you bothered to act—and very well, too!—the part of a loving bride. Could it be something to do with Glenappon?' he surmised mockingly, his wine-laden breath warm against her skin. 'Stay with me long enough to get a child and then buy me off with Mackay money?'

Fiona gasped at his shrewdly accurate barb, twisting her head in his painful grasp, growing still when his fingers dug into her scalp all the harder.

'Ah, I thought so,' he muttered with bleak satisfaction, a hard glint coming into his deepset eyes as he went on softly, 'And what if you've started throwing your money around prematurely? It seems the least I can do is to make sure that your plans have the desired ending!'

'Roderick, please. . . .'

Her breathy plea was disregarded as he dragged her head towards him and his mouth arrogantly came down on hers with a savagery he had never shown before. Numb panic sent her brain reeling, her hands scrabbling uselessly at his shirt front under the loosened dark jacket. Belatedly, she realised that no one had ever made her feel this helpless before, that she had always been in command and her wishes respected. But Roderick was no anxious-to-please young American with an eye to her father's hotel empire. He was a savage Scot with the blood of warriors in his veins, a blood that had been inflamed by the wine he had taken, a blood roused to a primitive seeking for domination over the woman he had married.

Just when violence had melted into the warm and sensual seeking for love, Fiona couldn't afterwards recall. All she knew at the time was that as Roderick's mouth gentled on hers, his hands seeking the sensitively responsive parts of her body that he knew so well, her pulses quickened and the familiar traces of desire rose in her throat and threatened to engulf her. The hands she had pressed rejectingly against his chest now felt blindly for its heart-pounding warmth, and the slender line of her hips seemed drawn to his as by a magnet.

A soft groan broke from him when she moved against him, and his lips left hers and traced a punishing path to the vulnerable depression at her throat. Fiona's eyes closed as she murmured his name over and over again, her hands reaching up under the cover of his jacket to stroke the tensed muscles of his back.

'Roderick . . . oh, Roderick, I——'

A peremptory rap at the door brought her eyes flying open, but Roderick took time only to raise his head a little way and shout thickly, 'Go away!'

'Is that what I'm to tell Jean McLeod, who's asking to speak to you on the telephone from Edinburgh?' Catriona's insolent voice came clearly through the panels.

The muscles at the back of Roderick's neck tensed as he stiffened, his eyes looking directly into the stricken blue orbs of Fiona. If he left her now, she vowed through the chaos leaping tumultuously through her, she would know for sure that it was the other woman who held his heartstrings.

But, dear God, he couldn't . . . he wouldn't. . . .

His arms still around Fiona, he turned his head and looked blindly at the door. 'Tell her I'm coming.'

A strangled gasp broke from Fiona, and he looked round at her, his voice huskily regretful as he promised, 'I'll be back very soon, don't go away.'

Damn him, damn him, damn him! Fiona thought savagely as he walked to the door with a steady gait that belied the effect of the spirits he had consumed. And damn the woman who always knew that he would say, 'I'm coming,' whenever she beckoned.

Moments passed while she ran the gamut of emotions from anger to hurt pride. Was it always going to be like this, men wanting her not for herself but for who she was? Would she never know the joy of being loved for herself—as Jean, who had nothing but herself to offer, did?

She became aware that her trembling lower lip, still soft from Roderick's traitorous kisses, was caught painfully between her teeth. 'I'll be back very soon', he had promised, expecting her to be waiting for him as if she were the Sultan's choice for this night . . . well, she wouldn't be here.

After her preliminary dash to the door, caution stilled her feet to an unhurried walk as she went across the vast hall to the staircase, conscious of Catriona's red-clad figure at the desk although the other girl kept her head lowered over a stack of papers as Fiona passed by. Roderick, his back to her as he talked on the telephone, was oblivious to her presence too. Mounting the stairs with a purposefully unhurried gait, she caught a snatch of his conversation.

'Of course you have to come! It's the only way—what? All right, get as far as Aberdeen and I'll come and meet you there.'

A lock had been installed on the outer door of the suite, and Fiona turned it firmly behind her, then leaned back against it, trembling.

The unmitigated gall of it! Insisting that his—his mistress attend the gathering meant to celebrate his marriage to another woman! Couldn't he at least have waited until she had shaken the dust of Glenappon from her feet before bringing his lover to replace her?

CHAPTER NINE

AWARE, next morning, that Roderick was busying himself somewhere out on the estate, Fiona took a walk round the borders of the loch, recalling her father's wistful recall of catching feisty silver salmon when she saw a solitary fisherman in a rowboat at the far side of the unrippled water. Achingly, she wished that he had lived longer and that they could have fished here together. . . .

But it wouldn't have made any difference. Uncle Fergus had left Glenappon and all its fishing rights to Roderick, the son of his second wife. Perhaps it was just as well that James Mackay never knew that his beloved home had passed into the hands of a man who had no blood ties to the Mackays. As well too, she reflected, stepping with her heavy brogues in the marshy land before the wide sweep of purple heather began, that he hadn't known of his daughter's marriage to that usurper of his home grounds. His Scottish temper would have flared had he known that his daughter of the Mackay blood was taking second place to a woman who had no real ties with the Highlands. Isabel, at breakfast an hour or so ago, had made the situation perfectly clear.

'I'm so glad Roderick married you, my dear,' the older woman had said with fervent conviction. 'He was infatuated with Jean McLeod—Jean Sinclair as she was then. They lived next door to us in Edinburgh, the Sinclairs,' she explained, 'and the three of them—Roderick, Andrew and Jean, were inseparable. Roderick made a big drama, in the way of young men, of being brokenhearted when Jean chose to marry Andrew, but I really think it was a case of hurt pride. And now I know,' she had patted Fiona's hand and smiled with romantic mistiness, 'that he was right to wait for his own true love.'

Fiona couldn't resist a sour comment. 'But Roderick has asked her up here for the gathering, so I presume——'

'Nonsense, my dear,' Isabel cut in with more loyalty than truthfulness. 'He just felt sorry for her—he's such a softhearted boy,' she added fondly. 'He could never see anyone left out of things, not even the little boy of our cleaning woman. Why, he——'

Fiona had tuned out of the lavish praise Isabel heaped on her son, her mind turning instead to the soft tap of his fingers on the suite door the night before.

'Fiona?' he had asked tautly, 'are you in there?'

Her breath would not have been audible through the thick panels, but she had held it anyway. 'Fiona!' he had persisted in a peremptory voice that made her flinch. 'Let me in, I have to talk to you.'

Still she said nothing, conscious that his hard-packed bulk would have made a considerable dent against even the stout wood of the panels had he chosen to exert himself. But he didn't—no doubt

regretting the presence of hotel guests who would
have been avidly interested in an exchange
between the Laird and his new wife.

'What did you say?' she cut into the older
woman's enthusiastic accounting of what was
about to happen that night.

'What? How long the gathering will go on?'
Isabel smiled wryly. 'I've known such celebrations
to go on until the small hours, with everybody
singing the old songs, their throats well oiled with
drink. Of course, as Fergus grew older——'

'No, I meant the dress for it,' Fiona cut in. 'Did
you say everyone wears tartan for it?'

'Well, yes, of course,' Isabel explained as to a
backward child, 'and very grand it is too when the
hall is filled with the colourful swing of the tartan.
Mind you, not all men's knees are fit for the kilt as
Roderick's are. . . .'

'What about the women? Do they wear plaid
too?'

'Certainly. Not the kilt, but a long dress in the
clan colours.' A stricken look came suddenly into
Isabel's eyes. 'But you won't have one, will you?
Oh dear, why didn't I think of it long ago when
Roderick first suggested the gathering?' She
seemed genuinely worried by what seemed a minor
catastrophe to Fiona. 'Perhaps we can find
someone who would lend you something suitable,'
she looked doubtfully at Fiona's slenderly con-
toured figure.

'No, thanks,' Fiona returned hastily, remembering the borrowed weeds for her uncle's funeral. 'I
have a tartan skirt that will do.'

Later in the day, the tartan skirt reflected a
blandly unauthentic image in the full-length
bedroom mirror. The soft white wool of the figure-

moulding sweater above it was the genuine article, woven in Scotland, but. . . .

A soft knock sounded at the outer door of the suite, and Fiona went on stockinged feet to answer it. Roderick had gone hours ago to meet his Jean in Aberdeen, and Catriona wasn't needed at the reception desk during the dull afternoon hours.

It was Rena who came hurriedly into the room bearing a large white cardboard box, which she placed on the low table bordering the plushly upholstered blue and white sofa.

'This just arrived for you,' she said, dimpling as she smiled and straightened. 'Personally delivered by the owner of The Highland Shop in Edinburgh. I doubt if many of her customers get that kind of service!'

Fiona stared at the package with its discreet coat of arms and simple inscription, *The Highland Shop.* 'But I didn't order anything from there,' she said, puzzled.

'Maybe it's a surprise from Mr Roderick?' Rena suggested over her shoulder as she hurried back to the door.

Slowly, Fiona took the top from the sturdy box and gasped at its contents. Like a dream answered, there was everything for the evening ahead. A lace-ruffled white silk blouse, its long sleeves caught in a wide band at each wrist, lay atop a simply styled but expertly stitched long dress with a vee at the bodice to accommodate the froth of lace from the blouse. The dress blended wide bands of green and black and blue ... to her shame, she couldn't recognise it as the Mackay tartan, but felt it must be. Unexpected tears rose to her eyes.

Roderick must have ordered this for her during those first few idyllic days of their honeymoon.

But when had he had time to order the perfectly right clothes for the gathering?

How had the seamstress known her size? she wondered as she held the long dress to her figure in front of the mirror. And how———? The bustling air of movement outside the suite cut short her conjectures and sent her fingers busily to the task of removing the clothes that seemed unbearably bland beside the authentic hues of her clan tartan. Tomorrow she would take the flight that would immerse her in the familiar world of commerce . . . tonight she would be the daughter of James Mackay, the wife of Roderick Cairns, enacting the fairytale drama set in the Highlands of Scotland.

The red-gold of her hair swirled about her shoulders as she descended to the already crowded hall, voices gradually quieting as awed looks were directed to the staircase. It was a re-run of that day when she had come down this same staircase for the funeral of her uncle, Fergus Mackay. But this time Roderick made no effort to spring gallantly to her side and lend her support in a frightening situation.

Fiona was more frightened, more desolately detached from the battery of stares directed her way than she had been then. Only Roderick's face stood out from the gathered assembly, and that was grim and hard under the dark blue search of her eyes as they swept from face to face.

On another man, his clothing might have seemed overdone, but on him the jacket of green velvet that sat comfortably on his broad shoulders, the vest of tartan over a white shirt and the kilt that reached to the mid-point of his knees seemed superbly right. He looked the perfect Highland gentleman, and the woman beside him in her white full-length dress and sash of yellow, black and red tartan looked perfectly at one.

Roderick moved forward, his buckled shoes set off by the dark green of knee-high socks, coming to the foot of the stairs as Fiona gained the hall.

'You look beautiful,' he complimented starkly, extending his arm with grave courtesy. A tense twitch of the muscle at his jaw told Fiona that the gathering would be as much a trial to him as it was to her.

Drawing her arm through his so that her fingers rested on the soft velvet with its underlay of sinewy muscle, he led her to where Isabel stood slightly apart, watching them with moist eyes.

'Mother,' he introduced formally as if they had never met before, 'this is my wife.'

It was as if he declared the fact for all to hear and challenge, but Isabel simply stepped forward and kissed Fiona on both cheeks, one generation given way to the next.

'Long life and happiness,' she said softly, 'and may you both love each other always as you do now.'

The words brought the sting of tears to Fiona's eyes, but Roderick was leading her on to Lady Carstairs, who unbent enough to smile as she wished them well and waved them on to the waiting estate people, who shook hands shyly and murmured their good wishes.

'Aye,' a rough-haired tenant farmer twinkled roguishly when her hand rested momentarily in his, 'the pair of you should have bonny lads to carry on at Glenappon!'

A wild flush rushed unexpectedly to Fiona's cheeks, but Roderick only nodded and moved her on to where the blonde Jean waited expectantly.

'This is someone who is very anxious to meet you,' Roderick smiled for the first time without strain.

Fiona thought she might faint as they reached the calmly smiling Jean, clean and wholesome-looking in her white dress with its slash of tartan round the waist. The cool blue of the fair woman's eyes swept over Fiona appraisingly, narrowing as they reached waist level.

'This is Jean McLeod,' Roderick introduced, the smile still in his voice. 'We've known each other since we were children.'

Jean's small and cool hand reached out to Fiona's, her voice holding a hint of laughter when she said, 'We've met over the telephone, but Roderick was being so secretive about your dress that I couldn't introduce myself properly then. He wanted it to be a surprise for you for the gathering,' she explained to Fiona's blank expression.

'Oh. I see.'

She didn't, and a quick glance up at Roderick's openly smiling face did nothing to enlighten her. What did her dress have to do with——?

'Anyway,' Jean laughed, 'tonight you're a credit to The Highland Shop, although,' she looked accusingly up at Roderick, 'her waist is narrower than you described. But all in all, the dress is a good fit.'

'I'm not the best judge of women's measurements,' he allowed, his eyes running over the ruffle of lace and tartan, 'but I think I didn't do too badly. And you did a wonderful job, Jean, in such a short time.'

Fiona looked bewilderedly from one to the other as they discussed her dress impartially.

Something wasn't quite right. By now Jean McLeod should be flaunting her undying hold over Roderick, her childhood sweetheart.

'Thank you, but I think the credit should go to Fiona ... and don't forget, by the way, that The Highland Shop doesn't only specialise in tartans—we have a very good selection of day dresses and——'

'I'm sure Fiona will remember that when she needs more clothes,' Roderick interrupted hastily, drawing Fiona away as if glad to escape from the blonde woman. 'I want to have a word with Craig Jameson.'

Fiona's legs moved obediently for a step or two and then stopped functioning completely. The sudden drag on his arm made Roderick turn, a question in his eyes.

'I—I'm sorry,' Fiona gasped, her face paling to the colour of Jean's gown. 'I——' Tearing her hand from his arm, she turned on her heel and plunged desperately through the loudly chattering guests, ignoring their astonished glances as she fled to the far side of the hall, finding herself outside the half-hidden door of the study and slipping inside.

Even her heart's beat seemed loud in its cloistered silence, her chaotic thoughts like screams in her head. Oh no, what had she done?

Roderick hadn't cared about Jean at all! He had seen her that first night of the honeymoon because he had been planning a surprise for her, Fiona, from Jean's clothing store. Buying a dress for this night, the gathering to celebrate the start of their life together at Glenappon. A life she had spoiled for ever by her stupid suspicions.

'Fiona?' he asked quietly from the arched door. 'Are you all right?'

She swung round and gave him an abstracted stare, then shook her head. 'No, I'm not, and I haven't been for a long time, it seems. I——' she shrugged and spread her hands helplessly, 'I've really messed everything up, haven't I?'

'Have you?' he asked quietly, leaning back against the door and regarding her thoughtfully.

'Wouldn't you say so?' She bit down hard on her lip. 'I ruined the most beautiful experience in my life because—oh, what does it matter!' She turned away to hide the quick rush of tears to her eyes, and found herself spun back to face a suddenly furious Roderick.

'It matters!' he gritted. 'That also happened to be the most beautiful experience in my life, and I'd like to know why you feel you ruined it for both of us.'

She stared into his eyes for a frozen moment, then whispered, 'I thought you were in love with— with Jean.'

'*Jean!*'

Pulling away and going to stand with her back to him, she drew a quivering breath. 'I know now how stupid I was to think that, but when I saw you that first night in Edinburgh, coming out of the hotel with her, kissing her, getting calls from her after that. . . .'

His breath was expelled in an angry explosion. 'If I was in love with Jean, as you thought, why in heaven's name would I have married you?'

'Because my name is Mackay!' she rounded on him, anger glinting through the tears. 'Can't you understand? No one in my whole life has ever wanted me for *me*—they wanted James Mackay's daughter for what she could give them, not because they cared. Even—even you. . . . She turned away again, her slender shoulders shaking under the bright tartan dress, her hands held up to her face.

Gentle hands came down on her shoulders and Roderick pulled her back against him. 'Oh, Fiona, do you not know how I've wanted you since that first time I laid eyes on you at Edinburgh Airport? You were the answer to my prayers, a beautiful woman with all the pride of the Mackays in your red hair and the sparkle in your blue eyes. That night I lay and watched you sleep and it was torture for me not to touch you, and I knew then I had to have you as my wife. I dreamed about you,' his cheek rubbed softly on the silk of her hair, 'and of holding you to your promise to marry me the day of your uncle's funeral. I gave you time to get over your father's death, and then I came to New York for you.'

He turned her in his arms so that she saw the grimace that passed over his face. 'And I found you with a man whose deepest knowledge of you was that you had changed your perfume.'

Fiona gulped and gave him a tremulous smile. 'I think he must have found out a lot more than that about the woman he's marrying in three weeks!'

'What?' Roderick held her away from him and frowned. 'I thought you said——'

'I said he'd mentioned marriage,' her smile deepened, 'not that he was marrying me.'

Slowly he pulled her back and gave her a fierce look as he reached his fingers into her hair and tilted her head up to his. 'Just as well for him, Mrs Cairns.' His mouth touched lightly on hers, moving gently over it, then deepening as his arms firmed around her and pressed her to the hard length of him. Fiona's hands slid up round his shoulders with their covering of soft green velvet to stroke the thick hair at his nape, and Roderick lifted his mouth a fraction from hers.

'You'll not lock the door tonight?'

She shook her head. 'No ... never again.'

'Oh, I've no doubt you'll want to when things don't suit you,' he chuckled huskily, 'so I think I'd better have another key cut.'

The door opened, letting in a gust of noise from the hall, and Isabel popped her head round. 'Oh dear, I'm sorry to disturb you, but I think you and Fiona should start the dancing off, Roderick. After all, the celebration is for the two of you'.

'We'll be there in a minute, Mother, there's just something we have to settle here.'

'Och, come away, you've a whole lifetime ahead of you to settle whatever it is.'

Fiona smiled into Roderick's glinting eyes. Would a lifetime be long enough?

Harlequin® Plus

A WORD ABOUT THE AUTHOR

Elizabeth Graham was born in Scotland, grew up in England, and today makes her home in British Columbia, Canada's Pacific province. Her first Harlequin, *The Girl from Finlay's River* (#2062), was published in 1977.

She is passionately devoted to her profession, which she finds a solitary one. And yet she asks, "Who can feel really lonely when a book's characters fill the mind's eye in the colorfully exciting parade of incidents and scenes that go into the weaving of a Harlequin novel?"

For Elizabeth Graham, the pure joy of creating people from the imagination cannot be equaled. "I move in a world that changes constantly," she enthuses, "and characters become so real to me that I regularly fall in love with my current hero. Only reluctantly do I relinquish him—and that's halfway through the next book."

Among Elizabeth's favorite activities is the reading of Harlequin books, and she expresses the feelings of many readers when she tells us why. "Problems," she observes, "which we all experience to a greater or lesser extent, are forgotten when I lose myself in another author's work and live for a while in her magic world. These problems are still there when I finish the story, but somehow the book's happy ending spills into my own life, and I'm better able to cope with life's ups and downs."

HARLEQUIN CLASSIC LIBRARY

Great old romance classics from our
early publishing lists.

FREE BONUS BOOK

On the following page is a coupon with
which you may order any or all of these titles.
If you order all nine, you will receive a FREE
book—*District Nurse*, a heartwarming classic
romance by Lucy Agnes Hancock.

The fourteenth set
of nine novels in the

HARLEQUIN CLASSIC LIBRARY

Great old favorites...
Harlequin Classic Library

Complete and mail this coupon today!

FREE
BONUS
BOOK

Harlequin Reader Service

In U.S.A.
1440 South Priest Drive
Tempe, AZ 85281

In Canada
649 Ontario Street
Stratford, Ontario N5A 6W2

Please send me the following novels from the Harlequin Classic Library. I am
enclosing my check or money order for $1.50 for each novel ordered, plus 75¢
to cover postage and handling. If I order all nine titles at one time, I will receive
a FREE book, *District Nurse*, by Lucy Agnes Hancock.

- ☐ 118
- ☐ 119
- ☐ 120
- ☐ 121
- ☐ 122
- ☐ 123
- ☐ 124
- ☐ 125
- ☐ 126

Number of novels checked @ $1.50 each =	$_____
N.Y. and Ariz. residents add appropriate sales tax	$_____
Postage and handling	$_____.75
TOTAL	$_____

I enclose _____
(Please send check or money order. We cannot be responsible for cash sent
through the mail.)
Prices subject to change without notice.

Name _____
(Please Print)

Address _____
(Apt. no.)

City _____

State/Prov. _____

Zip/Postal Code _____
Offer expires February 29, 1984

30856000000